AURORA MONTREALIS

MONIQUE PROULX

AURORA MONTREALIS

STORIES

TRANSLATED BY
MATT COHEN

DOUGLAS & McINTYRE
TORONTO VANCOUVER

Douglas & McIntyre
1615 Venables Street
Vancouver, B.C. V5L 2H1

The author thanks the Quebec Ministry of Cultural Affairs.

The publisher acknowledges the support of the Canada Council for the Arts
and of the British Columbia Ministry of Tourism, Small Business and Culture
for our publishing program.

Canadian Cataloguing in Publication Data

Proulx, Monique, 1952-
[Aurores montréales. English]
Aurora Montrealis
Translation of: Les aurores montréales.
ISBN 1-55054-258-3
I. Cohen, Matt, 1942- . II. Title.   III. Title: Les aurores montréales.
PS8581.R6883A9713 1997   C843'.54   C97-931028-8
PQ3919.2.P763A9713 1997

Cover photo-illustration by Brett Simms
Design by Michael Solomon
Printed and bound in Canada by Metropole Litho Inc.

CONTENTS

GREY AND WHITE

I'M WRITING to you, Manu, even though you don't know how to read. I hope that things are going great for you and that the rocks of Puerto Quepos stand to attention when you go swimming in the sea. We're moved in now. We have a sofa, a new mattress, two tables, four straight-backed chairs almost the same colour and a marvellous refrigerator that could hold a huge number of tortillas. I sleep on the sofa, beside the marvellous refrigerator. Everything is going well, I often get woken up because the refrigerator snores but the road to riches is filled with noises that hold no terror for the brave. On the other side of the window is a lot of pavement and grey houses. You can see an endless stream of cars, never the same one twice, Manu, and I'm not just boasting.

It's called Montreal. It's northern and extremely civilized. All the cars stop at all the red lights and after a certain hour it's forbidden to laugh. There are very few *guardias* or dogs. The word "northern" means it is colder than you can imagine even though it is only November. Right now I'm wearing three Montreal wool sweaters on my back, and Mama is warming herself in front of the open door of the oven that belongs to the stove which is, like the refrigerator, big and marvellous. But we'll get used to it, no doubt, the road to riches is a cold one.

This month, it's still going to be impossible for you to come, but don't despair. Every night before I go to sleep I make as though I'm stroking your head, it helps me dream about you. I dream we're catching lizards together and you are running faster than me towards the beach at Tarmentas and the sea is waking me up with its terrible groaning, but it's the refrigerator.

Here there is also a sea. I went once with my friend Jorge, and it is very different. The Montreal sea is grey and so modern that it doesn't smell of living things. I told Jorge about you, I gave you an extra ten kilos so he'd admire you more.

Here is how I spend my weekdays. There are things like getting up, eating and sleeping which I do often and quickly. Two grocers on rue Mont-Royal pay me to deliver things. I already know lots of English words, like *fast, fast*. The rest of the time I'm at school: it's a big grey school with a grey pavement yard and one tree, which half broke when I climbed it. The time spent at school is the worst, naturally, I try to remember only what might be useful later.

On Sundays, Jorge and I smoke cigarettes and we walk and walk. In Montreal you can walk for a very long time without ever seeing the horizon. We were doing that once, looking for the horizon, and we got lost and the *guardia civile* kindly drove us back to the house in a new car and I thought of you, Manu, because you love running after new cars to scare the tourists.

I don't want you to think life isn't good here, it wouldn't be entirely true, there are so many things I'm seeing for the first time, and the smell of richness is even starting to filter into our studio apartment. Yesterday we ate enormous chunks of beef, Manu, tender in a way you can't find in Puerto Quepos, and I'm sending you a well-wrapped sample. What bothers me the most, I can't lie to you, is the northern aspect of the city, and the grey, which is the national colour. As for Mama, what bothers her the most are store toilets, that's where she works and she is paid to clean them. You should see those stores. You would think they are villages except they are more civilized and have more things, you can walk around inside them for hours without having time to look at all the wonderful things we're going to buy ourselves as soon as we're further along the road to riches.

But I have to tell you about this. The big event. Mama was the first to see it. She was cleaning the refrigerator and by chance she turned to the window. She gave a startled cry—I rushed to see. For a long time neither of us could move; we were looking outside and laughing like crazy.

The beauty, Manu. The white beauty falling from the sky, absolutely white where before it was grey. Ah, live long enough Manu, stretch out your dog's life long enough that I can bring you here to be with me and play in the snow.

THE PASSAGE

So HERE is what the room was, once rid of the embellishments that had masked its true nature: a miserable birdcage. Everything was small and ugly: the carpet, which seemed to have been attacked by entire colonies of starving moths, the washed-out pink walls, the plain pine furniture, and the blind—what a horror!—in glazed paper you would have thought had been dipped in blood, though she had chosen it herself, centuries ago. Three months, to be exact. The unimaginable was thinking that she had lived for years in this sinister place, paralysed in the stupidity of childhood. But now that was over. Never again would she sleep alone on a futon narrow as a gynaecologist's examining table, never again would she look through the window at the skinny catalpa whose skinny branches her father used to draw together with nylon stockings.

Gaby sat on the floor and pulled her diary out from under the carpet. After several fruitless attempts, this was the only hiding-place that had escaped the suffocating attentions of her mother. She opened the small black notebook at random: "November 21st, 1991. Today Pierre Valiquette didn't look at me during biology. I am too fat. Life is ugly. Tonight find a way to kill myself with lots of blood." Childish. She turned a few pages and came to something more amusing. "The principal made me come to his office, locked his door, pulled down his pants and made me do things I can't even confide to you, dear Diary." This was obviously nothing but a stratagem designed to reward her mother's indiscretion; her poor high school principal, timid and ascetic, was only brave enough to look over the girls' heads, as though in search of their haloes. The success of her stratagem had far exceeded her hopes. Gaby remembered the scene with delight: her parents trapped in an impossible situation, so horrified by the depravity and debauchery that threatened their only daughter that they would have to admit they were in the habit of violating her privacy by reading her diary.

Gaby struck a match and held it theatrically to the note-book. Where she was going there was no more room for schoolgirl rambling, it was time to burn these dull bits of her past. And while she was at it, she added the Michael Jackson poster that had been hanging over her bed for two years to the auto-da-fé.

"Gabrielle, it smells like fire," her mother moaned from the other side of the door.

The two of them were pretending to be busy in the kitchen, she with her nose in the casserole smelling of stale leeks and liver, he in the grip of a sudden and suspect attack of hygiene, his hands busily whisking invisible crumbs from the tablecloth.

"Good," Gaby said, coughing.

Her overnight bag was heavy, she set it down while they said something—"Goodbye" or "Slut" or "What have you got against us for the love of God!"—various scenarios were possible, she just had to stay calm. Through the window she could see the old Renault parked against the sidewalk, and David's thin arm waiting calmly on the steering wheel.

"Aren't you at least going to have something to eat?" her mother finally tried, without looking at her.

"No," Gaby said.

"NO THANK YOU!" her father immediately corrected, in a nasty tone of voice.

All this time he was ferociously dusting the tablecloth—
"He's going to sprain his wrist," Gaby said to herself, and she
felt an unwanted fit of giggling making its way up her throat.
But she wasn't taking them by surprise. For two months they
had known about her imminent departure for Montreal, and
the week before, when they'd watched her moving her personal effects, everything possible in the way of futile and bitter
remarks had been made. There was nothing left for them but
this childish and stubborn desire to block the normal course
of events, to throw themselves uselessly in the path of the torrent.

"And no job," her father ground out. "No hint of a job in
sight."

"My God, my God," her mother sighed. "Is your apartment heated at least?"

"A little freshly hatched community college graduate. And
she thinks she's better than the others."

"Do you have a refrigerator? Do you at least have something to eat?"

"I can see it all now. Parties, parties, then unemployment.
There's thousands out of work in Montreal with wads of
diplomas, and you, poor innocent…"

Gaby waited patiently, her eyes fastened to David's arm still
resting on the steering wheel, serene as a mountain. In the end
they were unable to say the things that needed to be said,
though behind their dried-up protests she could hear them:
"Gabrielle, we love you, we're going to be worried about you."
They were tangled up in the all-encompassing pride that was
their trademark, please never let me be like them.

"You're still a minor, do you realize I could stop you, make
you, force you to…"

"To what?" Gaby asked calmly.

She looked him in the eyes the way she knew how, neither

challenging nor arrogant, a clear and straightforward way of saying: I am me, it's me you're talking to—and her father finished off his sentence with an indistinct mumble. The truth was that she had always known she was stronger than them, and smarter, and they knew it too, which was the limit of what they could tolerate. Without adding a word her father went into the living-room. For a moment her mother continued to punish the leeks in the casserole. When Gaby came up to kiss her, her mother offered only a half-cheek stiff with tension.

Outside, freedom had the colour of late afternoon and smelled like the stuffing of old Renault seats. Smiling, David took hold of Gaby's bag.

"How was it?" he enquired.

"Nothing. Let's go."

She saw her mother, shoulders a bit hunched, pressed against the window, waving awkwardly, a little girl's wave. Suddenly, with an unbearable sharpness, she saw that her parents were old and would one day die. She in turn opened the door to call something out, to wave her hand, but her mother had disappeared.

Despite David's efforts in painting the small four-room apartment on rue de Lorimier, he hadn't been able to cover over the fact that it was a basement. Someone born and accidentally abandoned there might have lived his whole life without knowing he was on a planet supplied with light. Nevertheless, Gaby looked the apartment over with the triumphant air of an owner. It was all hers, this untouched territory on which she would leave her own marks, the way a cat would imprint its odour—and of course David's too, although she was already seeing David as a kind of harmonious ramification of herself. This wall dividing the living-room would have to be taken down; for atmosphere they would hang snapdragons under a few infra-red lights which would substitute for the sun and spread subdued light to the corners of the room; they would buy exotic fish with unpronounceable names that ate raw meat. She had seen some at the corner pet store and they were all incredibly beautiful. David listened to her talk, nodded his agreement with that slight smile on his lips that had first seduced Gaby and still made her faint. He was sweet through and through, the way others are ambitious or vegetarians. He was six years older than Gaby, totally broke, and focused the major part of his obsessive intelligence on studying political science—which would probably lead him straight to the welfare rolls, but you have to try to believe in something.

As they pushed the critical investigation into the bedroom, Gaby, feeling David's warmth behind her, suddenly turned round and, purring, pulled him down to the bed. Why had no one ever told her about this fabulous delirium of the senses, the body's fantastic and extravagant capacity for pleasure—like a race horse allowed to run free? In the name of what hypocritical virtue had this amazing news been suppressed? And while they entangled themselves endlessly, wound themselves together, galvanized by desire, Gaby observed her reflection on the metal lamp-base: her hair wild and pirate black with that provocative pink curl at the front she'd preserved from the punk era, but above all an expression on her face that she didn't recognize, furious with the heat of her passion.

David lit the candle. The rickety table was made from unfinished plywood, its lace cover speckled with holes, and the flowers David had bought that morning were hanging sadly over the lip of their vase because he had forgotten to put in water.

It was a beautiful meal.

"Let's start with dessert," Gaby proposed.

"Why?"

"Because that's what you're not supposed to do."

They did. They ate three-quarters of a sugar pie with a topping that tasted like turpentine and then, caught between nausea and ecstatic giggling, they held hands and let the candle burn. "My love, love of my life," Gaby said, and David, who didn't tend to declarations, contented himself with smiling and crushing her fingers, while a small interior voice, a flicker of lucidity, whispered to Gaby that there would be others, many others, who would love her as he did, other stages, other men, and this whole endlessly long journey ahead.

"Suddenly you seem sad."

"I'm not."

They went to bed.

In general, Gaby didn't like the night, which returned the sentiment. But this couldn't be like other nights because Gaby was definitively leaving the tame country of celibacy, she had, what a miracle, her lover licitly pressed against her warm flank, already asleep and happily giving out a baritone snore. David had slid his arm under her neck; the warmth from their two bodies blended together. This should be it—happiness, or at least sleep. Gaby watched him for a moment, a sideways glance because his embrace had her immobilized. He loved her, yes, but couldn't he love her from a slightly greater distance? She unfolded David's angular arm and tried to sneak to the left. David immediately followed, as though magnetically attracted, and Gaby found herself driven to the edge of the bed, trapped between the boiling heat of their bodies and the void. It was dawn before she fell asleep, after having mentally chosen the gigantic bed she was going to buy with her first paycheque from the job she was bound to find the next day.

There were at least fifteen of them sitting there, so stiff with their nervousness and not wanting to show it that they seemed to be part of their chairs. Gaby crossed the waiting-room watched by at least fifteen pairs of listless eyes, and went up to a bespectacled young man with light hair behind a desk, wanting to ask him a question. But with an air of pained disapproval the young man pointed at the clock on the wall; then, with a radiant smile, he pointed to the waiting-room. Gaby understood right away and, impressed with the efficacy of the non-verbal communication, she went and seated herself in the midst of the chairs and their occupants. With two or three exceptions, most of those who had ended up there, hoping for heavenly manna in the form of paid employment, were older than her. Gaby attempted to approach the girl sitting next to her, a short redhead who looked barely twenty years old, with slightly protruding eyes and a knee bouncing in rhythm to her breathing. The short redhead, stupefied at being spoken to, threw Gaby a ferocious look that Gaby interpreted as a warning: no one was talking, it was better to keep quiet. Perhaps you even got punished if you failed to seem petrified with anxiety while awaiting the sacred call.

During this time the employees, leaning on the half-walls that separated their offices, were exchanging cake recipes and discussing last night's television programs in an ambience of lively camaraderie that the crowd of indigents glued to their straight-backed chairs could only envy. Then it was 8:30, then 8:35, and gradually the functionaries began to function, and the lucky first person, who was neither Gaby nor the short redhead, was called by an employment officer.

Two hours later Gaby was telling herself there must be some mistake, or perhaps it was a case of total contempt, because she had been summoned to appear at 8:30, on the dot, yet whole crowds of people had been called before her; meanwhile others continued to arrive like some sort of locust invasion. Apparently this city was swarming with the needy. Then, after the coffee break, Gaby was told she was next on the list.

At 11:45 Gaby, dazed and demoralized by the long wait, met the agent who had been assigned to her case for all eternity. Her name was Raymonde Bernatchez-Lizotte; this was announced on a melamine plaque, doubtless intended for the unconvinced, placed on her desk. As well, on the desk, was a picture of a baby which must have been hers—same cross-eyed look—a Persian-cat calendar, a big cat-shaped ashtray, a bronze cat paperweight, a couple of artificial flowers apparently made from cat hairs, and Gaby's file. Raymonde took the necessary time to consult it carefully, perhaps even learn it by heart—it was only one page—before showing any interest in Gaby's physical persona.

"You have a college diploma in communication studies," she summed up with a discouraged sigh.

"Yes," Gaby said.

"How old are you?"

"Seventeen."

"Tell me, Gaby, why did you move to Montreal? What kind of job would you like to apply for?"

Gaby noted, without letting it show, that she had just gone down one notch in the universal scheme of things. This passage into condescending first-name familiarity had no doubt been brought on by her age; after all, there was no scientific proof that a seventeen-year-old, barely past puberty, was entirely human. In her firmest voice Gaby reiterated what was already spelled out in her file: that she would be interested in anything to do with public relations, editing, media communications, radio, television or computers, and that, moreover, she had strong organizational abilities in any field. Raymonde emitted a brief and sarcastic chuckle.

"You have to be realistic," she said.

In brief that meant that Gaby's professional aspirations, laudable though they might be, were of as much interest and relevance as the daydreams of a solitary worm. Into what delirious megalomania had she fallen, to imagine, first of all, that the kind of idyllic jobs she had described existed anywhere in this vast world, and secondly, even if they did, that she, a miserable little runt just hatched from the collegiate magma, possessed the necessary competence to get one?

"If I were you," Raymonde offered fraternally while looking at her watch, "I would continue my education."

Of course she would continue it, later, in a nebulous future that would not involve Raymonde Bernatchez-Lizotte, expert in professional and other placements and proud of it. But in the meantime, was it a crime to occasionally want to buy fresh oysters, or to sometimes see a show instead of just reading about it in the newspaper?

"Of course, times are tough. Look on the bulletin board, there are a few things, baby-sitting, also a job selling shoes, I think, but there are a lot of applicants. I'll call you if anything new comes up."

That was all. That was, monstrously, all. She stood up, offered Gaby a weak handshake, looked her over with her crossed eyes and then let her out into the work area, emptier and more disorganized than before. Good luck, goodbye, good riddance.

No one was left in the waiting-room. Feeling it was hopeless, Gaby inspected every notice on the bulletin boards, sinking ever further into the shapeless fear that was forming in the pit of her stomach. And what if the universe, closed as an apple, had no space for her, ever, anywhere? What if she was just one among so many others, naïve and born too late, condemned to have her gifts atrophy, condemned to anonymous mediocrity? Suddenly she stopped at an announcement stuck between two requests for truck drivers: PR PERSON SOUGHT FOR SMALL FILM COMPANY. Of course, they required a degree and three years' experience and, worse, the opening had expired the day before. Resigned, Gaby started to leave the room. Then she came back, tore the advertisement from the bulletin board. After all, closed as apples may be, worms are quite capable of getting inside.

The building was low to the ground, encrusted in centuries of dust. Without anyone questioning her, Gaby went to the top floor, where the film company occupied a few shabby rooms. She got a distracted glance from a girl buried under mounds of paper.

"Who's taking care of the new PR job?" Gaby asked brusquely.

"John," the girl muttered, waving vaguely towards the end of the hall.

Gaby knocked lightly, went in, closed the door behind her.

"I'm here for the job," said a voice from inside her, a voice she hadn't heard before. "I'm the one you should hire."

The man straightened up behind his desk, cold as a curse.

"I don't know who you are, but please leave immediately."

When David came home from the university at the end of the day, he found the living-room plunged in shadows and Gaby, eyes serenely open, gazing at the ceiling. He came close to kiss her.

"I found a job," Gaby told him with a placid smile. "I start Monday."

What was this, what was she saying, how had she done it, and for a film company, yet? Had she told her parents, bought champagne, sounded the trumpets of victory? Gaby went outside to get some air while David, wild with pride, dared to telephone her parents, whose ostracism he found difficult to bear.

Summer was slow in coming; leaden clouds trailed across the sky, ready to burst open at any moment. In the middle of the street, two little girls were kicking at a ball and, just to amuse themselves, swearing loudly at each other. How predictable life suddenly seemed, a game for the under-endowed, perfectly decodable. In the end, she'd only had to go through the old ritual, take off her blouse and her skirt with that very certain look, just a question of minutes in the end, quite unimportant. He hadn't protested for long.

And while the little girls, hysterical and fragile fledgelings, ran down the sidewalk and disappeared, Gaby felt all that remained of her childhood leaving with them.

PLAYING WITH A CAT

H E I S walking along escorted by the sun, women smile at him, he smiles at children, every step launches him into a new adventure full of fascinating characters. Here, he will be happy. Here, he is at the heart of a luxuriant garden where people are to be plucked like fruit. Just a while ago he had an espresso with an Italian, drank retsina with a Greek, he has unknown brothers everywhere wanting only to laugh and to weep with him. He is immersed in the love of humanity and Montreal, and when he looks up at the impressive Stadium flagpoles he feels protected and welcomed as though by a village clock. The girl lives there, somewhere near the Botanical Garden. This evening he will telephone her, he can already taste the pleasure of hearing her stunned silence when he says, "It's me, Pierrot."

Gaily he climbs the spiral stairways at the corner of Saint-Hubert and Marie-Anne—he's been living here for two days now and it's already the historic home where his future is being constructed—and at the top he waves so cheerfully to the grumpy old lady shaking out her dustcloths on the neighbouring balcony that she gives him a startled smile.

The cat is dozing in the middle of the sunlit living-room, an old Buddha chewing over her previous lives. She opens her eyes slightly and two dazzling green beams consent to follow Pierrot's movements. Just a couple of words—"Hello, FatThing..."—and right away she's on her feet despite her corpulence, then on Pierrot's feet, twisting her small lion's head about with adoring humility. She nips him, and sometimes she scratches him as punishment for the hours he has left her alone, or for the next time he will, and afterwards, purring like a harsh four-cylinder engine, she licks him because he's hers again, her game has finally been returned to her.

The romance between them is old but still seductive. The cat, of course, is the one who does the seducing, because since ancient times the job of cats has been the domestication of man through a strategic alternation of burning advances and icy retreats. It works, it's called the art of love and war, and cats practise it more skillfully than do women. For example, in the last thirteen years Pierrot has had many women but only one cat.

The outside world abounds in treasures and disturbing odours which eventually end up inside. Today, FatThing is curiously sniffing at what Pierrot has brought home—a stuffed cat for the girl, wrapped in tissue paper for herself— but being also more unpredictable than a woman, she turns away without tearing anything apart and goes back to her Pharaonic slumber.

Pierrot sits and drinks a beer while looking out at the window and the landscape of spiral staircases disappearing into the twilight; then he eats, alone but as though in a couple, without feeling any lack. He watches his cat sleep and he thinks about women, some of the women he's known. Living with women could be nice, everything sweet and beautiful in the world is theirs, but they love anxiety, they cherish it so much that they endlessly invent reasons to be anxious. Anxiety leads to the reproaches that drive love away, anxiety withers even the youngest of passions. Do you still love me, what are you thinking, why don't you call? Anxiety creates the questions that grow from nothing into monsters that become real. There are so many ways to fly through the air, so many acrobatic trips, but women inevitably choose the path of gravity.

Pierrot thinks about the girl and his hand, unbidden, goes to the telephone. He has decided to move to Montreal for her sake, but he would have been equally willing, equally enthusiastic, about moving somewhere else—or not at all. Places have no importance, what counts is human warmth and the feeling of going forward while staying in the same place.

Her mother has assured him that the girl won't slam the door in his face. Her mother says she is moving towards a certain peacefulness, thanks to her therapy and her support group. Why should he be afraid? He'll get her to smile across the barbed-wire fence she's insisted on putting up between them. That's what he has always been best at doing—getting through people's barbed-wire defences in order to give them pleasure.

On the fourth ring the girl's voice appears with a regretful, breathless, mistrusting "Hello...," as though she were saying, "Now what do you want out of me?" And at that, all of a sudden, something unexpected keeps Pierrot from speaking; a jumble of images washed along by the small, surly voice of the girl drowning in a river of feeling that should instead be filled with laughter and ease. She repeats "Hello?" and instantly guesses who is keeping silent at the other end. "It's you," she says, "is that you, Pierrot?..." He manages to laugh, so that his silence can pretend to be a game. "How do you know?" he jokes. "How do you know it's not your boyfriend calling...?" The girl doesn't even smile. "I don't have a boyfriend," she says. "And anyway I've been expecting your call for two days."

The girl is twenty-five years old, which makes him forty-seven. The girl is a hundred and right from the beginning she's looked at life like an old hag who's seen too much to go for what glitters. With people like her, playful conversation can be dangerous, but Pierrot has few fears. He leaps into the void; soon everything he says is coloured by an irresistible twist of humour. Gradually she relaxes her surveillance, finally she begins to breathe normally again. Then abruptly she interrupts to ask what he is doing, right now, and why he doesn't come to her place instead of making these dizzy speeches over the telephone. "You're just steps away from Mont-Royal, so you can take the Metro." She gives him exact directions, as though he were a dysfunctional child. "Go towards Côte-Vertu, you get off at Berri-UQAM, then switch for Honoré-Beaugrand and get off at Pie-IX. Have you got that?"

There aren't many children in the subway, and there are few signs of childhood among the adults who sit there as though felled by some disease. The stuffed cat, huge on Pierrot's knee, inspires no curiosity. Perhaps they take it for a fantasy, a tired end-of-the-day hallucination. Pierrot remembers that he doesn't like subway trains and buses. In those places people's humanity finds itself suddenly endangered, and in the ferocious jostling of the crowd it's every man for himself. For example, opposite him, a women with sunken eyes is fearfully avoiding his smile. Pierrot has made her his target because women never manage to plug all the holes in their armour. He fixes his stare on a small fold of skin, the place where a sag marks the wounded frontier of her mouth. He looks at her as though he would like to kiss her exactly where she hasn't been kissed for a very long time. Her inner alarms sound, but then waver. She glances at him, frightened. He smiles at her. She looks away but she is already lost, she turns back to him—how can she resist the imperious call that has resonated through the ageing bodies of so many women?—she turns back to him and her eyes are brilliant with youth.

And now, outside in the cool darkness, Pierrot admires the Olympic Stadium, for which the admirable citizens of

Montreal have been happily paying for ever. This building, which looks like an expired Sputnik, fills him with a sharp joy; this edifice is the city into which he is going to slide like a cunning rat, he will go to games, from up close he will examine the roof at the origin of the saga reported in the newspapers— a pitifully modest saga, of course, on the appropriate scale for Montreal's collective dramas. But first, the girl. The girl has never liked hockey or baseball games, never liked to play, and just a few minutes from here the girl is waiting for him like a strict grandmother.

There are no coincidences, the house she chose—the house that chose her—is an amazing evocation of their brief life together. It coils its cast-iron stairways up three storeys of blood-red bricks worn away by age, and in the small, well-kept flowerbed, nostalgically aspiring to prove the existence of life before concrete, grow basil and almost-ripe tomatoes—exactly like the ones that must be protected from squirrels, earwigs and the girl, who was always unable to resist forbidden people or fruits. Struck by memory the way others are by amnesia, Pierrot kneels in front of the sacred tomatoes that carry time in their perishable bodies, he prepares to pick one when a voice falls on him from three storeys up. "Don't do that," the girl tells him, "the owner doesn't want anyone touching his garden." She is suspended in the void above him, her liquid hair falling down like the flowers of a sparse clematis. If he were taller, if he had the stature of one of those mythical fathers in whose shadows children can bury all their fears, he could touch her face and know the expression in her eyes, but all he can see is a black shadow, a deaf crow towards which his lilliputian voice, impotent and inept, is rising. "Hello," he says.

"Hello," he repeats when he finds himself opposite her in the intimidating light of halogen lamps and white walls. He holds the stuffed cat out to her. Nothing soft, nothing mellow or indirect in her apartment, she stands erect in the centre of her empty living-room like a guerrilla confronting the enemy in a clearing: no one will surprise her from behind, ambush her from suspect thickets. When she takes the cat a trace of a smile passes across her emaciated features, but she keeps it only briefly in her arms, then sets it down and says in her mother's disillusioned voice, "So, you never get any older."

"Never," replies Pierrot.

He takes her by the shoulders and kisses her, on the hair because she has turned her head, he tries to hold her against him but she is so thin she slips out of his arms, supple as a willow branch. "Would you like some tea?" she asks, fleeing into the kitchen.

Something murderous has happened to the girl, but she has survived, and now her eyes glow with the stoic flame of those threatened from within. She is sitting beside him, on the white sofa that blends into the immaculate living-room, an austere sofa made to keep the body upright and the mind alert to life's dangers. Even when she is beside him, cold and silent, completely absorbed in absorbing green tea, he can feel her burning, consuming herself, threatening to collapse beneath the weight of her inner ashes. Where to start? What shortcut will enable him to meet her in the place where she's put herself? "I'm doing well," she says before he's found anything to say. "I'm better than I was, I've been sober for six months." Her hair is like his, a bushy black mass that makes her pale face, glowing with its own separate existence, into a dark-framed cameo. She pushes her hand through her hair, the way he does before revealing a surprising secret. "I'm happy to see you," she says without looking at him, and Pierrot puts his hand on hers, which is shaking. Quietly, she pushes it away with her icy fingers. "I'm happy to see you because there are things I want to say to you," she says, in a careful voice that demands respect and a respectful distance.

He listens to her, serious on the outside but inside perplexed and amused, because for someone who never liked to talk the girl is talking a lot, and her words come wrapped in packages with labels he doesn't recognize. He hasn't really talked with her for five years, what's called talking, just a few telephone mumblings she was always quick to cut off—of course in five years there have been many revolutions, but so few people, to tell the truth, so few people are capable of really changing. "I've changed completely," the girl says, "coke and alcohol provided me with an identity that wasn't really mine. Now I have to confront my inner emptiness without crutches," she adds, with a tightening of her mouth that passes to her shoulders, like a signal from her pain commanding her to be quiet. Which she obeys. In this silence filled with all the inner emptiness not yet confronted, Pierrot suddenly notices the girl's back, frail and grooved like a bird's, and it is on this change that his eyes stumble and hallucinate, poor girl, so round when she was small, poor little girl, what inner emptiness cost her her feathers? "I didn't have a father," she takes up, her voice filled with new energy. "It is more painful to mourn a living and irresponsible father than a dead one. My father never watched over me and kept me safe. My whole life I've been without someone to keep me safe," she concludes, for once looking him in the face, her expression almost cordial, so much so that Pierrot might be tempted to smile and nod his head, even to await more interesting tidbits about this father who was too dangerous to keep anyone safe. But she is staring at him and hoping for a reaction, a wounded protest as if, in the end, he was the problem. Pierrot stirs his cold tea with the embarrassed feeling of having been mistaken for someone else. What she wants from him is impossible to exhume, doesn't exist in him. "I don't hold it against you," the girl finally sighs. "For a long time I did."

The tea is cold, so it could be time to get going, time for a farewell kiss, time to go do something cheerful. Pierrot takes hold of a stray limb and lifts the girl to her feet. "I'm taking you dancing," he decrees. Her face is crumpled in dismay, and then once again she has that look from another era, pitying and crafty, the look of Wisdom confronting the Infantile. "What are you trying to run away from?" she asks Pierrot.

Once again she's down in the rubble, on all fours, searching through the charred remains. He promised her so many things, in the Middle Ages of her childhood: to take her to New York, show her the Nile, give her a horse, unkept promises that struck home like a knife, killing lies so often repeated. "Once," she said, "I waited all night for you to show me the man in the moon, I stayed up all night waiting, and you never came, never…You promised me we would tame finches… You swore to me that there were crayfish in the bathtub…"

She has cracked apart, and from all her openings flow endless rivers of lava and bloody slag. Attentively he listens, he tries to understand. It must be a question of words, they don't talk the same language since they changed cities, she insists on labelling as promises what were only shared dreams, she accuses him of lying when he was only playing at inventing the unlikely. But he doesn't have time to translate into his own language because she has already moved on—with every floodgate she slams shut, she opens a new one. "When you sat me on your lap," she says, "you always made it so one of your knees was between my thighs." Pierrot, immobile and watchful, waits for her to continue. But she adds that it isn't serious, that it's the unconscious, by which she means the Oedipal, she talks to him about the Oedipal as though it were a personal enemy to be struck down and he listens respectfully.

Occasionally he tries to slip in a few bland words, an excuse, something to tell her he understands, but she pays no attention and he falls completely silent when he realizes that nothing he could say would ever be enough. What she wants from him, in the end, are neither apologies nor justifications, what she wants is for him to suffer too, she needs his suffering to reduce her own.

Why, in these immodest confessions she is brandishing in the bright light, is the problem never love? How can you be twenty-five years old without being lacerated by passion, devoured by desire? And suddenly it's as if she guessed Pierrot's silent hesitation, she stares at him with a new look, glowing with fervour, and when her voice returns it is thick with sensuous yearning.

"I've found Him," she says, smiling. "It took me a long time to admit His existence, but now that I know Him I love Him. Without the Supreme Being, life without crutches isn't possible. But the Supreme Being is capable of everything, once we hand over our life to Him." Pierrot looks away, seared by the harsh light in the girl's eyes. He remembers her biting intelligence, her precocious nihilism, and suddenly he is suffering, yes, more than from any other of her confidences; he suffers in silence while the girl, enlightened and ardent, talks about the Almighty. "Only the Almighty," she says, "is supremely capable."

He is the first to get up. It's only as he gets to the door that she thinks of asking after him, but only by touching on inoffensive territory. "Have you found a job in Montreal?" she asks. He says yes, Monday he begins working for the city. For a moment she looks at him closely, as though shocked by his capacity to find jobs, his good fortune, his powers of seduction. She says, "Me too, I'm also working for the city. A two-month contract." And she bites her lips while he, laughing, blurts out, "Maybe we'll end up working in the same group," then stops because he too is struck by these likenesses that appear without warning, their black hair, their almond eyes haunted by an inexhaustible hunger, their shared unwillingness to involve themselves in careers that could make demands on them. Too bad he didn't pass on the most important thing, the lightness of heart without which you stumble into life as though into a muddy trench, too bad happiness can't be inherited.

In the white desert of the living-room, Pierrot and the girl linger face to face, two exotic plants, two shrubs from the same family transplanted into hostile ground. The girl's voice is fragile again: "Tomorrow evening, to celebrate my six months of sobriety, there's a party at Cocomaines Anonymous. It's called a 'sharing.' I would like it if you came." She glances at him fearfully, adding that it's for eight o'clock.

"Of course," says Pierrot, "eight o'clock, I'll come." He looks for the exact words, the soothing ones that the girl's therapist must use to calm her anxieties; he doesn't find them. He says, directly, "I'm glad you're feeling better. I promise you, I'm truly happy." She looks at him and a corner of her mouth pulls up with something nasty, an uncontrollable sarcasm that she manages to hold back. Instead she throws herself at him, she punches him at the same time she's kissing him, a little ball of affection and rage, and finally he embraces her, submerged in a happiness he has never known.

The next day is a Friday, the last free Friday before the city makes off with his skills and his daily sweat. He gets up early so he can squeeze every possible ounce of enjoyment from the day to come. What he likes best of all is wandering about aimlessly, stopping at unknown cafés, daydreaming, alone or with others—daydreaming the way you sleep while outside life goes on constructing the miraculous twists we are destined to encounter. But before he thinks about going out, even before he gulps down a coffee in his kitchen stained by the first rays of sunlight, he sees that this morning of his last work-free Friday is missing something. He looks around, looks for what's missing. The cat. The cat isn't there, imperious, starving, overcome and delirious with happiness at finding him in the morning, winding between his feet as he tries to walk, hobbling him with her extravagant caresses.

He calls her: "Thing, FatThing." Nothing. He crumples some of the tissue paper he always leaves on the floor, producing irresistible rustlings. Nothing.

He finds her behind the living-room sofa, gathered listlessly in a position of attack, a non-functioning detonator. As his hand comes towards her head, her eyes follow listlessly. When he begins scratching her forehead, an amorous ritual to which she has never failed to succumb, she moves abruptly away from him. Pierrot doesn't insist. He leaves fresh water in a few strategic places around the apartment and he goes. Cats, like women, sometimes get into moods that are best avoided.

The day is so beautiful that it keeps slipping away whenever he tries to embrace it. He strolls through Old Montreal, he eats mussels and shrimps; humming, he comes back up boulevard Saint-Laurent; he sits down wherever women seem to be expecting him and for fifteen minutes he loves them intensely; he drinks litres of coffee and wine while exchanging banalities with waiters and waitresses, he buys the girl a necklace of transparent pearls that may, he hopes, bring light to her inner darkness. When he gets back to his apartment it's six in the evening.

On the living-room carpet he sees round stains, almost red, connected to each other like Tom Thumb's pebbles. He follows them to the bedroom, under the bed. The cat is there.

She has vomited everywhere. He scolds her a bit, for form's sake, to avoid more violent feelings. The cat, her eyes veiled, red foam at the corners of her mouth, is dying.

The heaviness of twilight floats through the room, fogging his mind. Again and again Pierrot looks under the bed, amazed. The cat he knows is alive, silky, has never played at dying. Where has his cat gone? What is this lifeless dull-coated beast with its blood-smeared head, ugly as a pain that won't go away, doing under his bed? Who finds it amusing to wreck such a beautiful day? A feeling of enormous irritation descends upon Pierrot, it makes him start scrubbing the carpet angrily. Suddenly, kneeling on the floor, he stops. The cat's tail, erect as an exclamation mark, comes out from under the bed as if everything were just a game. The cat's tail is a marvellous tri-coloured plume that he loves to rumple, and she always presents it to him with a courtesan's generosity because, from the tip of her tail to her cat's heart, she is completely his, lovingly enslaved. In a panic Pierrot gets up, grabs the telephone and calls all the veterinarians in the city for help. Very few respond to his appeal at this beginning of a holiday which is indifferent to the workings of death, but one of them says, "Come," and Pierrot runs, racing until he soars above rue Saint-Urbain to the edge of the Chinese district, where a veterinarian filled with the miraculous science awaits; Pierrot runs, in his arms an old sick cat who has only him to bring her back to life.

Veterinarians have all sorts of ways of concealing their miraculous science. This one is a small, nervous man who has obviously been abandoned by his clients. He shows Pierrot right into his cage-sized office—at the back of which a real live bird hops about in an even smaller cage. "It's a mynah bird," says the vet. "He can speak." He looks at the mynah bird as if waiting for it to confirm this. The mynah bird says nothing.

The vet listens to the cat's chest, weighs her, gropes in each of her cavities, mumbles curses when he learns her venerable age—thirteen years. He gives her a bit of serum to revitalize her, temporarily. Temporarily, he admits unwillingly, because she is fatally ill, with a combination of distemper, leukaemia and old age which—it is necessary to accept—can't be cured. He blinks under Pierrot's fixed and accusing stare. "It's not possible," Pierrot says. "Just yesterday she was perfectly healthy." The veterinarian clears his throat, addresses himself to the mynah bird with a voice filled with humility. "That's often how it is with cats, old cats. They are in good health and then, just like that, they're gone." He accompanies the "just like that" with the gesture of drawing a knife across his throat. Then he offers his tired sympathy to Pierrot, along with some pills to be administered every six hours to ease FatThing's desperate state. He even offers to keep her in his cramped cage for a few days, but nothing makes up for his horrible impotence and Pierrot, hating him, accepts the pills.

Now the cat rests against Pierrot's chest, soft and languid since having the serum, and her green eyes, stunned eyes, flicker at every car they meet, as though she's finally getting a bit of excitement from this return home. When Pierrot sets her down carefully on the sofa, in the darkened apartment, she emits the shadow of a purr before falling asleep.

Pierrot drinks several beers, turns on the radio, and soon he's drifting along with Neil Young in a sea of plaintive loves and uncomplicated feelings. Afterwards, when he starts to think again, the natural order of things seems to have been restored, everything is back in place. Animals are aesthetic but limited creatures, with primitive souls that don't require excessive attachment. It is unhealthy, doubtlessly degenerate, to feel for animals in ways that should be reserved for humans. When cats die, you replace them with other cats, or with dogs, even better travelling companions for a warrior.

Thirteen years. When he found the cat abandoned in a pine grove—or rather, when the cat found him, thirteen years ago—his hair hadn't yet developed white streaks, his eternal youth was entirely unwrinkled. Suddenly an unexpected pain passes through Pierrot. Beings cannot be interchanged. Each lost being is an irreplaceable loss. Living beings are not interchangeable, and it has taken him forty-seven years to have this devastating revelation.

At five in the morning Pierrot wakes up. He remembers. He remembers that he forgot; in the evening's torment he forgot the girl, the girl's celebration, the "sharing" he had promised to share. He calms down. Now that they're back together, she'll understand that we don't meet death every day. He waits until eight to call her. If he wakes her up, so much the better; they'll go to breakfast together, she will comfort him. She answers on the second ring. She wasn't asleep. Perhaps she never sleeps. For a moment she listens to him recount the dramatic details of his evening; then she interrupts him, deliberately, her voice so calm in comparison to his overexcited one— in her Olympian voice she tells him she doesn't want to see him any more, ever, either him or the train of lies that accompanies him everywhere. Then she hangs up.

An eternity passes.

Pierrot sits down on the floor, in the rustling tissue paper strewn all over the carpet. He feels something on his hand, a velvet caress. The cat is crouched next to him and is trying to get at his fingers across the irresistible barrier of crackling paper. Her eyes are sparking demonically, her cat's eyes that would sell her soul to play. Surely the effect of the pills, the temporary burst of energy that the vet predicted. Pierrot slides his hand under the paper, faster and faster, and the cat goes wild, she leaps about him, forgetting to retract her claws, with all her strength she attacks and shreds the paper; ridiculous and magnificent, she makes war by inventing an enemy. Pierrot can't help laughing, caught up in this game that annihilates the suffering; for a long time he plays with her, for as long as the reprieve lasts. Tomorrow she will be dead but today she is alive, tomorrow they will all be dead, but today they are playing, playing in the lightness of life for as long as life is with them.

THE POINTLESS AND THE ESSENTIAL

BEACHED IN front of the train like a man-eating whale, the bus had started to disgorge its insides: small crumpled beings emerged from the air-conditioning blinking their eyes, and among them Martine instantly recognized Fabienne, wearing her lop-sided hat. The hat undulated to the baggage hold, seemed to engage in a fierce struggle with some bare heads, then emerged triumphant from the melee with two bulging suitcases. Fabienne's face, at first vacant, became very anxious as it rapidly advanced towards Martine while trying to smile.

"I'm hungry," Fabienne called while she was still far away, long before they touched. "The trip was horrible, rude children shouted in my ears for three hours, the woman beside me stank of sweat, I should have taken the train, it was so hot, so many people, I'm so hungry, where are we going?..."

"Hi, Mom."

They embraced awkwardly. Fabienne smelled of cheap cologne and jam, the new-cut grass of the little Val-Belair bungalow and the mothballs from its cupboards. Martine was immediately invaded and shaken by phantom odours: a hot raw whiff of bog welled up from the Jacques Cartier River while wet clothes trembled on the clothesline, her father lit a pipe on the deck and suddenly it was summer, rustling with hay, crickets and sweetened tobacco. "You smoke too much," Fabienne was saying, "you smoke too much, it's dangerous."

Martine took the suitcases and started to drag them towards the exit. Fabienne walked beside her, zigzagging like a crab, her attention claimed by a thousand urban monstrosities—"My God! That girl with the pink hair!... Look, that man is almost TOTALLY NAKED!... Have you noticed, all the taxi drivers are black..."—but it was only once they were in the car, while they were going back up rue Berri in the killing heat of the afternoon rush hour, plunged suddenly into the heart of the wild stampede of animals bolting each for itself towards its den, that Martine rediscovered her mother in her full glory, the sawmill of emptiness, the incredible source of endless banalities. "Your brother bought a power lawnmower with a built-in insecticide sprayer, little Agnes got her hair cut like Madonna she's so cute, Mrs. Cayouette, you remember the woman who lives across from us with a port-wine stain on her cheek? She told me the other day that Mrs. Bigras—the new neighbour behind us who has an unbearable little mutt—claims I throw my dead leaves in her yard, can you believe it?"

Martine, dizzy with vertigo, was struggling desperately not to fall apart; maybe you could die of an overdose of meaninglessness, or at least be shrunken for the rest of your life, and she struggled to re-establish her interior silence while all sorts of screaming little animals—little Agnes power Madonna insecticide port-wine stain little mutt on dead leaves—snuck giggling into her ears. She risked a glance at her mother; Fabienne's face, anaemic with age and constant dieting, was fixed hungrily on rue Saint-Denis, but her attention was still directed inwards, towards the shallows of the lapping wavelets that made up her universe.

The moment she entered Martine's apartment, Fabienne demonstrated her utter helplessness. She had come to Montreal two years ago, when her daughter's stylish six-room apartment showed every sign of normalcy. Now she found herself in an immense white desert, ABNORMALLY immense and white, and she kept looking for the walls, the doors, the furniture, all those familiar things that clearly proclaim the civilized individual.

She finally came out with "Where's Simon?" in an alarmed tone that might mean: where did the walls and the only reasonable person in this place go?

"Come on, Mom."

Simon had vanished two years ago, at the same time as the walls and the ancient heaviness of existence, and Fabienne had been the first to know and had forgotten just as quickly. Martine didn't have the energy to scold her for her mistake. She'd had a feeling that this week would be hell, even before offering the masochistic invitation she'd known it, and now that her mother was standing before her, flanked by her eternal absurd little hat and her country-bumpkin suitcases, for once briefly silent, her premonition became a certainty: yes, the week would be hell.

With a little girl's daring, Fabienne found the courage to move forward in the loft, amused by the clicking of her high heels on the floor of this empty cathedral. She hurried to open the door that led to the toilet—finally! something a bit conventional—then another door that opened onto a small windowless room with a futon as its only furniture, bathed in a bluish light.

"Is this my bedroom?" she asked, terrified.

"No," Martine said, "it's my...it's where I meditate. Cogitate," she corrected, in response to Fabienne's stunned look.

Then they were in a rush to eat, because, when it came to taking in food, Fabienne's stomach demanded punctuality. Her mother would have preferred to do her gobbling in company, if possible in the midst of a jostling mass, but Martine had made a vegetable couscous that Fabienne, with her fierce passion for animal protein, sadly devoured.

Afterwards the whole evening stretched out before them, a stagnant unbroken calm of lugubrious hours waiting to be passed—and it was just the first. Fabienne was seized by a new fit of volubility; the idiocies of the abominable home tribe had once again reached glorious heights. Overcome by a cowardly resignation, Martine paid attention sporadically, once again staggered by her galactic distance from these tepid beings, her brothers, her sisters, stuck to cretins like themselves, who hated and feared anything that escaped Val-Belair. Fabienne was the most salvageable, but she was burdened by so many problems that Martine had always tried to escape. And Fabienne, as though horrified by the life her younger daughter led, never made any real attempt to find out about Martine. Martine was sinking into a resentful stew when Fabienne, on her own, suddenly interrupted the deluge to leap towards the larger of her voluminous suitcases.

"I just remembered!... I brought you a few little things..."

And from the entrails of her country-bumpkin suitcase she brought out jars of strawberry jam and plum jam, brandied pears, wild blackberry vinegars, home-made bread, gooseberry wine, hazelnuts, maple sugar, brioches, a hand-braided rug, two sweaters, gloves and a red wool balaclava decorated with fluttering black Canada geese. And as she proudly displayed her treasures, her eyes glowed with authentic maternal love, which can't be bought or faked, which leaves a vertiginous hole when it's missing, which can only be responded to, finally, by yielding.

The hat had a feather and, under that feather, a big mobile mouth that twisted like a flag in the wind. "I want the bird," said the hat mouth, "bring me the whole bird!" "Quiet," Martine ordered, "you'll wake my mother." "No," the hat cackled, its mouth curving into a sneer, "the one I'm waking up is you…"

Martine opened her eyes; she saw the hat at the far end of the loft, momentarily reduced to silence. Beneath the hat was Fabienne.

It was eight in the morning, the October light had barely started to make a pale rectangle on the unpainted floor, and there was Fabienne completely dressed, sitting up straight in front of the television, which she was watching without the sound, her hat on her head, ready to plunge into whatever exalting adventures the city had to offer. A small mumble from Martine was enough to make her mother leap to her feet, turn off the television and, a smiling stick of dynamite, cast herself upon Martine.

"I've made you some pancakes, they're on the warmer. It's weird, your television has the same programs we do. Where are we going this morning?"

This "where are we going?" was filled with a terrifying energy. Mornings, Martine got up carefully, to unify her interior fluids; she did half an hour of tai chi and half an hour of meditation in the blue room; she ate fruits, grains, oils and dairy products in exact proportions. Then a kind of warm serenity would begin to course through her veins, and she felt, quite physically, her brain sparking with well-being and inventiveness. And this inventiveness was necessary because she wrote very serious texts for avant-garde magazines and educational television, texts Fabienne had never dared to try reading because she was afraid she wouldn't understand anything. Thus this week would be in no way comparable to the serenity of her solitude, and there was no doubt it would take a couple of months for Martine to recover completely.

"Mrs. Chapleau made me a little list," Fabienne said. "You

know, Mrs. Chapleau, Monique's husband's cousin's wife who has a sister who often comes to Montreal."

Out of her purse she drew her little list and a camera. The list was made up of the places and tourist sights that Mrs. Chapleau's sister-who-often-came-to-Montreal considered absolute musts for a tourist from Val-Belair.

"The botanical gardens, Beaver Lake on Mont-Royal, the musée des Beaux-Arts, the Olympic Stadium with the elevator that goes up, the Biodome, rue Sainte-Catherine but not too late at night, Old Montreal because they sell T-shirts with Montreal written on them, the CBC studios while they're taping an episode of the new Lise Payette serial..."

Martine, overwhelmed, thanked God that at least Saint-Joseph's Oratory had been omitted from the must-see pilgrimage list: this Mrs. Chapleau's sister, nasty though she was, must not be very religious.

"The chic boutiques on rue Laurier," Fabienne continued studiously, "the smoked meat at Saint Laurent on Schwartz..."

"At Schwartz's on Saint-Laurent," Martine corrected weakly.

"....the Mont Royal cemetery, the English district, the..."

Martine burst out laughing, a laugh full of misery and despair.

"The English district?"

"Of course!" said Fabienne. "You know it, in the west, *West Moon* it's called..."

Yes, it was so easy to imagine, Fabienne with her little hat and her camera suddenly arriving at the homes of the residents of Trafalgar Heights, in Westmount, hammering the solid gold knockers of a few three-million-dollar cottages to inquire politely, "Are you English?... *May I take a photography?*"

"But there are English people all over!" Martine exclaimed. "I can introduce you to some in the apartment downstairs if you want."

"Dinner at L'Express on rue Saint-Denis," Fabienne continued, annoyed, "a shushi dinner at the Japanese restaurant..."

"Sushi is raw fish, you wouldn't like that!"

"Why not? I've never tasted it. Raw fish is good for the heart."

She put her list back in her purse and waited patiently while her daughter agreed to show her a few of Montreal's marvels. Martine girded herself in stoicism and they plunged into the city.

In the subway, which Fabienne had absolutely insisted on taking, they did not pass entirely unnoticed. To claim her territory, Fabienne clung to the edge of her seat. At each station, despite Martine's endlessly repeated directions, Fabienne's excited voice quivered through the car: "Do we get off here? Is this where we get off?" A Vietnamese man came and leaned near her seat; when she noticed him she was terrified, but then, reassured by his smallness, she ended up asking him if he missed his own country. At the Berri-UQAM stop, near the exit, she paused to wildly applaud the musician—a pathetic wretch who was torturing a mandolin until it cried—and then gave him the magnificent offering of ten cents.

Having decided to minimize her pain, Martine led her mother to the Botanical Gardens, a high point of harmony and calm more in tune with her own inclinations. Fabienne admired the orchids but was mortally disappointed that she wasn't allowed to take home a little clipping. And after half an hour she found that the clusters of vegetation, with the way they evoked the country, were getting boring to look at. So they moved on to the Olympic Stadium cablecar. At the top Fabienne insisted on tossing pennies into space for good luck—without a thought for the pedestrians below, whose heads were being pelted with the stern face of the Queen of

England—then was overcome by a fit of vertigo, forcing them to make the trip back down, several hundred metres, on foot.

There were some other epic bus and subway journeys, an expedition into Old Montreal to unearth those horrors most suited for export to Val-Belair, a discreet pass along rue Laurier to take a look at various forms of wastefulness, and then Fabienne was hungry.

Martine's combativeness had been so reduced that they ended up at the Mikado, where they ordered "shushi" and sashimi. Fabienne welcomed these amusing oriental intricacies, but a nervous stab of her fork into her *uni maki* convinced her that the cute little things were still alive. She paled.

"But this is absolutely raw!" she gasped, horrified.

"Really!" Martine sniggered without an ounce of compassion.

Her mother, who had known worse adversities, hailed the geisha with an imperial wave of her finger.

"Could you put these back in the pan for me?" she simpered. "Not long, just five or six minutes..."

During this whole time while Fabienne criss-crossed and devoured the city, her mouth was ejecting words at a staggering rate, she was talking and reality shrank as though sucked away inside, she talked and life became a hopeless anecdote from which all mystery had been for ever and ever removed. She talked and she held herself against Martine, always grabbing her arm, rubbing against it like an obscene lover. And this contact was even worse than the constant talking, was the most horrible thing possible, it said: you and I, so unlike each other, are bound for life. It said: never forget this, Martine— no one will ever love you as much as I do.

And Martine, crushed, knew it was true.

The third day, someone from educational television called Martine, who was officially on vacation, to ask her to prepare some urgent paperwork; never had work been welcomed with such enthusiasm. So on the third day Martine harnessed herself to her computer the way you go to the beach, her heart purring, and Fabienne had to visit the marvels of Montreal by herself.

Sighing with apprehension, she looked through the window at the downtown skyscrapers. How to get there unharmed and back again without being trampled by metallic brontosauruses, locked into labyrinths, attacked by cutthroats? Martine drew maps and routes, wrote down her address, made her repeat the directions like a slow student. Then Fabienne went out, her lop-sided hat on her head, her purse gripped tightly in her hands. From the window Martine watched her knock over a fat man who was going in the opposite direction, before disappearing, terrified, into the unknown.

At the end of the afternoon of this third day, Martine's doorbell rang, and when she went to the door Fabienne was there, flanked by two uniformed policemen. She came in without a word for Martine. Not even looking at her, she went straight to the bathroom. The policemen stood politely at the door. This is what happened, one of them explained, while the other smiled at his own inner fantasies: there had been a subway breakdown, total darkness and the usual panic, you know how it is, and this lady hadn't gotten over, you might say, the shock, they'd had to pull her out by force from under the bench where she was crouched and go through her papers to find her address, maybe she should see a doctor or have a little something to drink for medicinal purposes—for the something to drink the policeman had a kindly, confident smile.

Fabienne remained tense all evening. She refused to eat or take off her hat. She stayed on her bed, stiff and resisting, and to everything Martine said she shook her head. Eventually she stretched out on the bed, her eyes fixed on unknowable visions. Martine sat beside her and massaged her temples. Fabienne's skin was grainy and yellow, like old photographs.

In the middle of the night, Martine woke up. The big room was quiet; then she became aware of something in the midst of the silence, an infinitely faraway stain that was spreading in small wet sounds.

Behind the closed door of the meditation room, Martine found her mother curled into her futon. The bluish light blurred Fabienne's outlines; nothing was visible but her crumpled clothes, gathered into a ball, unobtrusively moaning.

"What's wrong?"

The moans swelled to fill the room, a magma through which one word emerged.

"Scared," moaned Fabienne, "scared, SCARED..."

Timidly, Martine came closer to her mother. She smelled of animal sweat and pain.

"Faby's scared," her mother said distinctly, "oh, Faby's scared..."

Terrified, Martine looked at her. She was incapable of dealing with this kind of thing, she was going to have to call a doctor, some stranger who would know how to bring her mother's confusion under control and make her rational again. Now Fabienne was blurting out complete sentences, in this lost voice that was like a childish relative of her own.

"Faby's going to die, don't want to, don't want to die, Faby doesn't want to die..."

"You're not going to die, come on, Mom..."

"Mommy," said Fabienne, her mouth twisted unhappily.

"Mommy, Faby's got the little bug, the little black bug, Mommy…"

That was what they had always called cancer in Martine's family; her father had died of that unnamed thing ten years ago, that little black bug had nibbled away at his lungs. ("You're smoking too much," Fabienne would say, "you're smoking too much, it's dangerous…")

"MOM! STOP THAT!"

"Mommy, Mommy," the baby Faby kept saying, clinging to Martine, "Mommy, please, I don't want to, don't want to die…"

She pressed her grey head with its thin hair against Martine and suddenly she became again what she'd never stopped being beneath her lying exterior shell, a frightened little girl crying for help. Martine calmed herself and remembered what her mother used to do, take the child by her shoulders—oh, the so recent sweet times when all the cares of the child Martine had dissolved against those shoulders—take the child Faby in her arms and rock her, rock her, yes, put all the bugs to sleep…

When she got up the next day, Fabienne put on her hat and announced that it was time she went back home. Her voice was strong, her eyes were only slightly evasive. She apologized for the night before, an inexplicable blackout, a touch of the old claustrophobia, her maternal uncle used to have the same problem, "Edward, you remember?"

And in the car taking her to the bus station, she told the terrible story of the horrors of that subway stopped in the humid darkness, a woman was weeping in a foreign language, a man stank of urine, a drunk had started laughing: everything was normal again, every detail just a detail, and Martine remained silent, frightened by what was left unsaid. Out there, concealed behind every car, the little black bug was watching them go by. She had to ask the essential question, the one that was tearing her apart inside: Is it true? Do you have It?

"Look," said Fabienne, "the geese are going south."

Standing near the platform, they watched the migrating birds in flight over the city. When Fabienne lowered her head, her expression was so serious that Martine knew she was going to say something, say something real, answer the silent question. Martine hurried to speak first, quickly, quickly, to fill the emptiness with words, no matter what, so long as they floated, light and deliciously pointless, to quickly smother anything that might destroy her innocence.

And Fabienne, her eyes glowing with relief, remained silent.

YELLOW AND WHITE

—————————

FOR *Ying Chen*

YOU WERE right, Grandmother, places are porous mirrors that hold traces of everything we are. When I was a girl, you and I used to look at the gardens from the other side of the Huangpu, in Shanghai, my eyes were too young to see anything but peasants and plane trees swaying in the wind, while your eyes dove down beneath the surface of trees and hurrying people to bring back invisible images.

Now I know that every place can speak, Grandmother, the gardens and streets of Shanghai, the streetcars and buses, the houses and mountains, even the stores.

My life-to-be in Montreal was revealed to me by a store, a store like an archipelago of overpopulated islands whose thick crowds are made up of objects instead of living beings, a store with a strange name that gives no hint of its contents: Canadian Tire.

I was planting dahlias in my new landlord's garden, and I wanted to prop them up with a stake. I went into this Canadian Tire just to pick up a metal rod or a piece of wood and it was three hours before I left, my mind stuffed full but my hands empty.

The things in this store, Grandmother, are in aisles wider than a small street, extend farther than the eye can see and would climb right up to heaven if the ceiling weren't in the way. They are red, grey, yellow, green, big, small, elongated, round or rectangular, and nevertheless they all look the same, and the more you try to distinguish one from another, the more they multiply and hide and melt together into one single enormous object with an infinite number of parts and no discernible use.

I tried to work my way into the store just as I would have tried to move through the crowds on Nanjing Street. But how can you move forward without a landmark, how can you know which direction to go in? So I stood frozen, my heart gripped by fear, while the shoppers swarmed around inside the store, going by me without seeing me, determined to get where they needed to go, to a certain place where a specific object awaited them. I've never felt more confused and anxious than at that moment, Grandmother, at that moment when Montreal seemed to me an indecipherable enigma for which I would never find the keys and the codes for survival.

Someone noticed my distress; a man came up to me and asked, in French-accented English, if he could help me. I answered him in French, which is the only North American language I know, but at that moment no language could have helped me describe an object whose name was unknown to me, and when I gave him a panicky "No, thank you" he unfortunately interpreted those words literally as an invitation to abandon me right there, instead of hearing them as the politely formulated beginning of a call for help.

Help did not arrive, nor would it. I took a few steps in no particular direction and then, Grandmother, although I don't know how to swim, I plunged into this solid and bottomless ocean until it closed around me. I carefully inspected every one of those sophisticated objects, made by the hands of artists or robots; one by one I examined the bits of metal and coloured materials to try to deduce which part of a house or existence they might belong to. At one point I recognized knives. There were a hundred and twenty-nine, of different shapes and sizes, and I was terrified to think that in this fabulous country there existed a hundred and twenty-nine ways of cutting and I knew only one. A little later I saw sixty-three dishes of varying depths, and I wouldn't have known whether to put rice or nails into them. Suddenly, even farther along, I saw shovels. Shovels, Grandmother, close relatives of the ones our peasants used to dig the earth on the other side of the Huangpu, and I hurried towards them, because where there were shovels there might be a stake to support my flowers, my poor dahlias that were being swept into oblivion by this torrent of nameless objects.

I found neither a metal nor a wooden support, but I did find forty-nine kinds of shovels, and eighteen kinds of a big tool called a Weed Eater, an enormous thing wrapped in plastic and perched atop the aisles like a king endowed with obscure powers.

That, Grandmother, was my initiation into Montreal life, in that almost faraway autumn when I was still a Chinese shrub newly transplanted to North America.

Since then, the St. Lawrence has become as familiar to me as the Huangpu, and my walks along Saint-Denis are as relaxed as those you and I used to take along the Bund. Since then, I have also learned just how much all of Montreal was contained in that store that frightened me so much, that store of muddled utility and excess.

Now, Grandmother, abundance is part of my daily environment. Here there are so many clothes of different colours and cuts, so many places to buy them, so many complicated ways to make a second skin to transform my appearance, that for a long time I thought I would never be able to choose a skirt. There are so many shows and restaurants, so many flavours of ice cream—but no bean ice cream—so many cars and things to sell and to look at. Now abundance no longer frightens me, and the too-much and the nothing are unavoidably joined. So much news arrives and then disappears from the papers and television that sometimes I feel as though I'm back in China, where there was no news at all and it was impossible to know what was going on in the world.

I no longer say "No, thank you" to signify "Yes, please." Here, everything has to be stated loud and clear; words and actions follow a quick straight line that has no room for the poetry of the unspoken. Now I am able to return the kisses of my Quebec friends, because only this excessive embrace will convince them that my feelings for them are real.

In this store where a Francophone spoke to me in English, there is also the reflection of the shifting terrain the languages cohabit here, the reflection of this polite battle that Montreal's Francophones dream of winning without fighting. With each day I speak French better, but each day I feel their mistrust. I remain a weightless shadow in the background. They are the only ones who can free themselves from their mistrust, the only ones who can conquer the ground that belongs to them already.

Now I am alone, Grandmother, like a real human being. No one shows me the way in store aisles or in life, no one puts a protective hand on my shoulder to approve or reject my decisions. Like the customers at Canadian Tire, I go directly where I believe I need to go, without waiting for support, and I am capable of walking past the overflowing shelves without buying anything. At first it's not easy to recognize, but this is freedom, that painful and magnificent thing called freedom.

In the meantime China has also changed. I read about it in all the news that surrounds me here. I know the Chinese drink more and more beer, have fewer and fewer dogs. I know the desire for money has spread its frenzy everywhere, right into the most resistant levels of the Party. I know Shanghai is bustling beneath the developers' cranes, is being surrounded by modern expressways, and that Pudong, with its financial towers and high-rises, has wiped out its plane trees and its peasants digging in their gardens with thousand-year-old shovels, has wiped away, from the other side of the Huangpu, the images that were born in your eyes. Perhaps one day there will no longer be a difference between being Chinese and being North American.

In the meantime, most of all, life has slowly pulled away from you, Grandmother, and you no longer see or hear the words spoken around you. Between us words were never necessary, and these ones will find a way to reach you. I wanted to reassure you about the fate of your little one before Lord Nilou takes you entirely into his kingdom. I have found my place, Grandmother, the place inside that gives me the strength to go forward, I have found my centre.

HELLO

THE TELEPHONE booth is on a small street without trees, without passers-by, without anything to distract the eyes or constrain the imagination. When he shuts himself inside it on Monday evenings, with his address book, he is able to forget all sorts of unpleasant things, beginning with his own existence.

He telephones. He telephones women he doesn't know, which puts serious limitations on the conversation and, admittedly, is a reprehensible act punishable by law.

He always proceeds methodically, because that is the only way to get anywhere in life. From the telephone directory he chooses twenty-six women's names, one surname beginning with each of the twenty-six letters of the alphabet. It's simple and it encourages diversity. He can tell the women by their first names—Julie, Carmelle, Zéphyrine—or by the childish habit they have of hiding themselves beneath an initial, as if that in itself were not a sexual indicator. Obviously mistakes can happen: the other Monday there was an M. Proulx who stunned him with his brutish and aggressive voice, and furthermore—ours is a difficult age—many men decide to call themselves Dominique or Laurence, to confuse the issue. But these remain isolated cases; the true problem lies elsewhere. Last time, he realized the cruel fact that Yanofskys, Zajomans and Winningers are rare, in fact just ample enough to supply a dozen more Mondays, which means he will have to rethink his method. Already, rummaging about in these barbarous Ws, Xs, Ys and Zs, he has ended up with foreigners, Germans and Poles who didn't realize that what they were getting was an anonymous phone call; that totally destroyed his pleasure.

When he has made his choice of the twenty-six presumed women of the twenty-six letters of the alphabet, he copies them into his notebook, because that way it's more intimate, it draws them together. He leans against the glass wall of the telephone booth, he puts down twenty-six quarters, he holds his open notebook in his hand like a kind of white flag.

He inserts the quarters. He dials the numbers. He waits. He doesn't say anything. He waits for the women to talk, the voices of women he has never met, rasping and delicate, disturbed and aggressive, faded and youthful, so many different voices that take him, though he doesn't move, to so many amazing places. Yet he knows he isn't some kind of pervert; for example, he never masturbates on the telephone. What attracts him is something else, it's slipping secretively into their lives beginning with nothing more than a tiny detail— the texture of a voice, two or three syllables, and he can imagine everything: their faces, their immediate surroundings, the exact details of their moods, the way they dress and eat and play with their cats.

They always hang up too quickly, saying nothing or screaming into his ear, or, worse, threatening him with a very painful castration. He doesn't see what he has done to deserve that.

When he has finished his twenty-six calls, he rests for a moment with his eyes closed before dialling the last number, the same one every Monday, the one he knows by heart and hasn't looked up in the book.

She answers. He doesn't speak, he tenses in a state of agonized expectation. At the other end of the line, her beautiful, harsh voice grows impatient: "Hello! HELLO!..." and he is always torn apart the same way when she hangs up without recognizing him, when she throws him back into the void from which she only briefly rescued him when she brought him into the world.

PUBLIC TRANSIT

HER RAINCOAT rustled stiffly as she jumped between the tracks. She didn't fall, which was surprising for a body so tall and uncoordinated. And now she stands peacefully, her purse hanging securely from her shoulder. She is doing as the others are doing, she is waiting for the subway—but not in order to get in, obviously.

The news spreads like stomach flu through the rush-hour crowd, everyone in the Berri station gathers at the platform to watch; people realize that they are witnessing, right before their eyes, the unfolding of a drama, and it makes them happy and excited, most of them have never seen a real suicide—in flesh and raincoat, as I was telling you.

A certain Conrad is among the crowd; he sells shoes at Pegabo and he's a little shorter than average, which means he is unable to see the show. But he instantly understands that something unusual is happening and he moves closer, like the others, trying to be part of the adventure. People are murmuring to each other like old friends; "She's in desperate straits," calls out a tall man who can see everything and has probably read a lot. Conrad manages to elbow his way to the front row and then he sees her. She is wearing glasses, is in her thirties, not too attractive, eclipsed by her ordinariness, and by the big black raincoat which fits her awkwardly. She turns her back on everyone, as though to state that this whole scene has nothing to do with her, then she slowly makes her way towards the black mouth of the tunnel, where the rumble of a moving train can already be heard. To see her like that, so peaceful, it's impossible to understand—she's not the type to have been disappointed in love, she's not the type to have been through anything, and maybe that's reason enough for her to stand resignedly in front of a homicidal subway train.

Someone near Conrad screams, "Somebody *do* something!" and Conrad, after a slightly confused delay, realizes that this hare-brained call has come from himself. Around him the others signal their agreement by nodding their heads fatalistically, yes, of course, something must be done, but what, what can you do about death and isn't it already too late, the train is coming, poor poor girl, poor children poor parents of this poor girl. The train is coming, Conrad doesn't want to be the one, he never did, the train is coming, its mechanical howl is rising like a fever, it's too late for the controllers, too late to discuss things with the girl and convince her—of what, in fact? Miss, life *is* worth the trouble, stay alive, miss, if no one loves you I will love you...How could she believe him, he who loves only men? Suddenly Conrad leaps into the trench and, without thinking, jumps on the girl, half knocking her out; his strength unleashed, he throws her onto the platform like a bale of hay and hurls himself after her.

Just then, out of the blue, a television crew appears in front of Conrad. Dazed by the spotlights, he is raised to the crowd's shoulders and applauded. The girl in the raincoat takes off her glasses and her raincoat. Underneath she is as beautiful as the girls in the before-and-after beauty parlour ads. She explains to Conrad that it was all a live televised test of everyday heroism, he is the winner, is he happy? Conrad is interviewed on "The Journal" and "Pam Wallin Live," he's on the front pages of all the next day's newspapers, Jean Chrétien gives him a tie, the Pope faxes him forgiveness for his sins, he gets the Legion of Honour and the St. Jean Baptiste Cross.

The whole thing makes Conrad sick. He has to change jobs

because women are harassing him—are you the one who's the hero, can I touch you?... Now he doesn't use the subway any more. He walks. And when he finds himself stopped at a red light, beside a blind man, for example, he doesn't help him cross the street the way he would have before, no sir; he gives him a discreet little shove so he'll fall on his face.

CITY DRESS

IT'S A place where things of beauty can rub shoulders without oppressing each other, in an environment that leaves each the necessary space to shine. The armchairs, in warm velvet and hollow tubing, are as blue as an unchanging sky. Beside them, plants embedded in vast urns believe they are in the tropics and throw themselves into extravagant flowering. The light comes from everywhere, solar even when it rains. On the small low tables, where glass is mated with real marble, expensive art books and cultural magazines are left out to be thumbed through, and replaced the moment even a shadow of a stain appears on one of the pages. There are few paintings on the walls, but those few proclaim their authenticity: one signed by Edvard Munch, a second by Edmund Alleyn, the last by Riopelle in his geese-and-storms period.

It's an island of good taste and harmony where wealth doesn't make itself ostentatious, as though, here, money has no importance. And yet, here, money is at the heart of everything, the master to be contemplated and followed, the ultimate destination of all thoughts and actions, for we are in a bank.

The people who work here have moulded themselves into the ambient aesthetic, and they go about their business silently, a sort of transparent extension of the decor. The director, with his long aristocratic neck, irresistibly evokes Modigliani, except when he opens his mouth. The tellers buy all their clothes at expensive neighbourhood boutiques, which takes up most of their salaries. The security guard must have been hired for the perfection of his moustache, which he waxes with a Daliesque nostalgia. How could a client fail to feel at ease in the midst of all this beauty, where even money has acquired a delicate odour?

In the way of clients, today, there are only three, because we are at that slow time in the afternoon, just before closing. One wicket is open, and in front of it the first client is muttering cabbalistic numbers to a silently acquiescing teller. The client is a slender young man for whom beauty is important; this can be seen in the casual way he dresses and, looking at people, fixes on the things they have that count. He is a director in the theatre, a sacred space where money is rarely found but which sometimes leads—when, like him, you have what it takes—into the world of television which dispenses cheques of five figures not including those after the decimal. He is ready for action. In this district where he's just moved with his actor boyfriend, the smell of success is already in the air, just waiting to be breathed by those who are ready for action.

The second client, who stands with his knees as straight as the crease in his trousers, is also a man, less young and more classic. He has already worked for several years as an endodontist, he has debts to match his revenues and a family that ceaselessly and energetically increases the former while eating away at the latter. By doing root canals, by sectioning the infinitely small and treating the infinitely rotten concealed behind respectable appearances, he has acquired, along with disillusionment, a scrupulous respect for minutiae and order. He never keeps his customers waiting and he appreciates that at least here he is not kept waiting; now another wicket opens to serve him and he moves towards it, his step springy on his high-quality sponge-rubber soles.

The lady who's left alone to wait has the kind of enduring beauty that tries to last a whole lifetime. Unseen are the wrinkles and white hairs that exist somewhere beneath the perfumed powders and salves, and so subtle are the weapons that no trace remains of the arduous battle against time. This lady is the owner of a nearby travel agency. She translates people's dreams into dollars and talks about Cairo the way others talk about the Laurentians. She travels frequently but, alas, the moment she leaves her own place she becomes terribly bored. Her therapist assures her that this is only an umbilical passage, and that sooner or later she'll come to terms with it.

The door opens.

He comes in.

By "he" I mean the thief, the crook, the no-doubt safecracker.

His eyes have that unmistakable dullness, and he has the shifty air of someone with a lot on his conscience. He's wearing workboots caked in filth, and his jeans are overfitted and faded in a way that has been out of fashion for years. His skimpy sweater shows a strip of chalk-white belly, probably fed with beer. He's young but he has had enough time to develop a liar's face, topped by lank hair and a forehead that is already sloping away from the disaster. It's an ugly mug.

He comes closer. Soon he will be entirely within the lady's perfumed aura, cooking up some criminal abomination behind her elegant back while pretending to wait his turn. The lady goes pale and would do even worse if a third wicket didn't mercifully open for her, leaving the ugly face in a non-existent line, isolated, at the centre of everything—the stares and the rising levels of adrenalin.

The Modigliani neck of the director elongates by a dramatic centimetre, the tellers' fingers tremble towards the alarm button, the young man of the stage wonders if he will dive beneath the wicket or, for the sake of posterity, play the most heroic role of his life, the specialist in hollow teeth mentally composes a heart-rending farewell letter to his wife and children, the lady tells herself she'd better not withdraw any cash, the security guard rests his hand on the pistol pressed against his thigh.

During this time, lonely as a wound in the middle of a face, he, the gangster, the young shark, lets his shifty eyes wander about, while imperceptibly his fingers creep towards the inside pocket of his sweater to pull out his weapon—a knife, a bomb; imperceptibly but with everyone watching, he pulls out a package of cigarettes. He lights one. In the strong light his fingers can be seen—dirty and stained red, with blood, no, with paint, red like on his workboots, because he's nothing but a worker, a dirty worker who smokes.

He smokes, in this bank where, as I was saying, an authentic Edmund Alleyn hangs next to a valuable Riopelle, whence for ages cigarettes have been banished with everyone's consent because it's no longer snobbishness, it's evolution; *Homo postnicotinus*, the most glorious link of this Quaternary Period, takes care of his physical well-being and his suburban transit system, goes jogging on Mont Royal, spends as little time as possible down below on rue du Parc, swarming with riff-raff, germs and lung cancers.

The accumulated tension, the fear of dying and being robbed of the most essential possessions, is suddenly transformed into a cold fury aimed at the glowing tip of that outlaw cigarette.

Despite his primitivism, he catches the hostile vibrations and quickly crushes the cigarette against the sole of his shoe, having failed to identify the elegant oriental vase placed in the centre of the room as an ashtray. Shoulders back, he moves towards the wicket just vacated by the apprentice director. His voice matches his eyes—evasive, breaking, perhaps simply intimidated.

"I want to cash a cheque," he says.

He pronounces the word "tcheque," and holds out a piece of paper neatly folded in half. The teller slowly takes it between her index finger and her thumb. The lady and the endodontist pretend not to hear this conversation which they are following intently. The young dramatist lingers, so he won't miss any of the theatrical possibilities of the scene.

"Do you have an account here?" asks the teller, with the weariness of someone who is always asking questions with obvious answers.

"No," he mumbles.

And since the teller looks as though she's about to give him back the cheque, his face crumples, he goes pale, this money is his, he has earned it, the red stains on his labourer's clothes show how hard he has worked, his voice rises foolishly, out of control, like that of someone who hasn't learned to master his primitive impulses.

"The tcheque is good," he insists, "it is, it comes from the big house just next door, from an architect, it has to be good…"

The teller holds the cheque out to him without saying a word, without even having unfolded it. All eyes are on him, the unpitying eyes of justice.

He takes back the cheque. He understands. There's no doubt that the cheque is good. He's the one who isn't.

HISTORY LESSON

I'M SITTING in the lobby of the Quat'sous theatre. It's jammed with the night's audience excitedly waiting for the doors to open. Here and there people begin unfinished prologues, the short plays-before-the-play that no spotlight ever catches. Two voices rise above the general noise, two men's voices behind me throw out the same word like an irritated mantra, like a missile incapable of reaching its target: "Montreal, Montreal, Montreal." The Montreal of one is accusing, sharp, with an accent that rises at the end: "You people who live in Montreal, you think Montreal is the whole world." The other lovingly rolls the "r" of Montreal, caresses it in saliva: "Yes, for we who live in Montrreal, everything that's important happens in Montrreal." The skirmish unfolds elegantly; light but essential, it warms up the cerebral muscles of the cultural warriors, it's a Nautilus workout for more heroic battles to come, it exercises the language of attack, keeps it battle-ready.

"Montreal monopolizes government cultural subsidies Montreal's painters Montreal's writers Montreal's playwrights grab all the institutional money as though no one lived outside Montreal Montreal wants to destroy all the regions other than Montreal Montreal Montreal. Montrreal needs help your survival depends on the survival of Montrreal all the regions should be happy to encourage and contribute to Montrreal's culture instead of indulging in petty jealousy towards Montrreal Montrreal is where the true test of survival of the French fact is taking place only in Montrreal Montrreal."

Suddenly I hear a woman's voice, tiny and miraculously audible, making its way through the silent gap between two "Montreals." What is she saying? A short sentence, modest and almost indifferent: "The same debate must go on in Paris, Toronto, all the cultural capitals."

That's worth a look. I just have to turn my chair, as in an experimental theatre.

One of the men is sitting down. The other is standing. The woman is seated between the two men. The two men are dressed as men, jackets and pants in dull autumn colours. The woman is dressed like a flower, sparkling and in full bloom as though ready to be pollinated. She keeps looking at the man sitting beside her, Montrreal; she is openly in love with him.

The two men recommence their discussion, the words making their way diagonally over her head, suddenly going right through her when their voices fall too low. Now it's the word "Quebec Quebec Quebec" that turns in the air, bouncing back and forth—not the city but the country—"the country that will become the future native land of our future descendants," says one. "A country so abstract it is a ridiculous utopia," says the other. "Kebek Kebek Kebek." For a moment she sits still, irradiated into transparency from both sides; then, slowly, she moves. She makes an amazing gesture: she lifts up her bare arms as though to arrange her hair, and she leaves them there, raised like a drawbridge, opening to love, passion, that pulses instead of quibbling. To return the man to himself, all men, especially the man sitting beside her, Montrreal-Kebek, she offers the possibility of life.

Bodies speak better than words, but what they say must be deciphered, whereas it's so easy to hear loud words taking up all the space. "Kebek should be able to impose the desire for Kebek on all those who immigrate to Kebek Kebek should rediscover its inner pride and propagate that pride outside

Kebek the only way is for Kebek to become a country…"

"Kebek mission impossible Kebek childish blind cause Kebek ungrateful wretched land what use having in the name of the country Kebek the same cultural impoverishment as before as today as always Kebek Kebek."

She draws back her naked arms and her useless gesture of love, she covers her proffered body in a tweed jacket and, taking advantage of a silent moment while they catch their breath, she says simply, "Let's go inside, the play's about to start."

They pass near me as though nothing serious has happened, she stabbed and they guilty of the crime. We go to sit down in front of the stage. Monstrous history, monstrous politics, monstrous masters of a world blind to love. We go to sit down in front of a stage, to imagine for a moment that life always wins.

RUE SAINTE-CATHERINE

THE BEST place for panhandling on rue Sainte-Catherine is beside the Desjardins complex, beneath the big sculpture that looks like either a flying horse or a two-headed bat, depending on the amount of white gin you've drunk. The site offers space, intimacy and visibility at the same time, and best of all, shelter from rain and sun, though sun is seldom a problem in Montreal. Fine-sounding sentences are engraved into the sides ("The society of tomorrow will belong to those who know how to unite," "Union for life not battle for life," "Unite to serve"), resonating like the uncles' sayings at the family gatherings you never had. It really is a good sculpture, comfortable as a front step, and if I met the artist who made it, I wouldn't mind shaking his hand.

It's my personal shelter, everyone knows it, even that creep the Louse, who just stole it from me.

The Louse is a total insect, with his small weaselly face, the way he wriggles about as though he has a tapeworm, and most of all his hypocrisy. He's not even a real bum; almost every day I see him coming out of UQAM and then he stands at the corner, arrogant as a rich man's son. He pulls a flute from his schoolbag, he weaves about to draw attention away from his terrible playing, and, I have no idea why, customers rush for him. He must take that at university, how to manipulate people and get their twenty-five cents, now that there aren't any more jobs maybe they give courses in the sneakiest ways of begging.

When I saw the Louse insolently standing in my spot,

someone inside me got mad. Someone inside me grabbed him by the collar, shook him until all his fillings fell out of his teeth and sent him flying on the sour notes of his flute to the north side of Bleury. I know him well, that someone inside me, he's the same one who scores as much at university as on a hockey rink, he's the one who makes his music not with a school-child's flute but with a big black god's sax, and when he plays the sax he plays so well, he plays until passers-by stop and give him their tears in the shape of gold pieces. I know him well, that someone. He's as elusive as a ghost, he disappears just when you think you see him, and even the best white gin can't make him come out from inside.

I didn't say anything to the Louse, who is younger and stronger than me; I went back up the east side of Sainte-Catherine to find myself another spot.

The competition is unfair on the east side of Sainte-Catherine, another kind of charity stops the customers and makes them want to take instead of giving. Between the Ultra Sex, The Sex Club, The Pussy, The Sex Coach, Club 281 and the pretty little things near rue Berger, your misery needs a truly exotic face to get any attention. Better to continue past Saint-Denis and set up in the small park before Berri, to try to hook a few customers coming out of Archambault's—they might still have some change in their pockets. But there too the competition is unfair. That fucking university spreads its young everywhere, and they play at begging between classes, trying to get together enough money to buy a car before the summer.

On a nice June ninth like this one—what's more, a night with a Stanley Cup Finals game—spectators emerging from the Forum might at least walk as far as my sculpture, and share the Canadiens' victory or defeat with me. Using what remains of my white gin I soothe my bitterness, I curse the east, from which nothing can come, and the Louse, who I will strangle tomorrow morning.

Well before ten o'clock in the evening I hear car horns and screams of joy coming down Sainte-Catherine, so I know our Glorious Ones are on the verge of finishing off the Los Angeles Kings. That makes me happy, really, even though hockey has become something very distant, a weird cacophony fogging the Golden Fried Chicken television screen when the owner lets me in to finish off the chips from the fryer. But you're not a man any more if you don't take at least a shred of pride in the Canadiens.

Soon, in a pandemonium of triumphant honking, the first cars pour out onto Sainte-Catherine, and I see I was wrong to worry. They come up here, up to me in my corner of the park, in their tricoloured sweaters they lean out their wide-open windows, shouting and throwing me handfuls of coins. These are the young, the fine and gallant young, may God preserve the young and their fabulous Canadiens. Others arrive, other cars and other horns and masses of fine young people leaning half-way out their doors, waving number 33 sweaters and John LeClair and Paul DePietro dolls and pictures of Patrick Roy with his eyes half closed like an imitation spy. And just as in a real parade, red helium balloons float above the hoods, "4 to 1" is written on them, that must have been the score, and soon people begin to flood into the streets from everywhere and still the Forum has hardly begun to empty. Oh, it's a great celebration, and I just have to move along the sidewalk with my arms raised, like them, to be showered in quarters and dollars. I shout, "Long live the Canadiens!" and together they shout back, "Long live the Canadiens," what a beautiful happy generous family we all are tonight, what an exceptional night, what a beautiful June night.

I don't know exactly when it begins to fall apart. I suppose there are limits to how much happiness or how many people Sainte-Catherine can contain, or maybe when it gets too strong happiness turns on itself like an angry cat. Already it can't grow any more, the mass of cars and faces, but it keeps on growing, it becomes a grimacing tide of triumph screaming out war-cries. When I shout, "Long live the Canadiens!" two huge men naked below their Canadiens sweaters stop in front of me and piss down on me from their convertible. All sorts of things are thrown across the street from sidewalk to sidewalk. A bottle of De Kuyper, empty of course, just misses my head. It's getting too heavy for me, I retreat to the depths of the park.

And then the music begins. A crystal music, all along rue Sainte-Catherine, a grand symphony of broken windows drowning out all the other voices. I don't understand anything I'm seeing. Omer DeSerres, the Hubert Aquin Pavilion, the Golden Fried Chicken, Archambault Musique—all the façades explode, blown down by the storms dressed as Montreal Canadiens. Alarms go off, a police car burns as though we were in a country at war. I watch the multitudes of young people howling and laughing as they attack the stores and I've never been so unable to understand. I don't know why these little lice with their cars and their houses to sleep in and their girlfriends to keep them warm need to throw their triumph through windows like rocks, why is it them with their places full of fine clothes and CDs who go into the smashed stores and take everything, why is it them and not me?

When I see the first guy coming through Archambault's smashed front window with a guitar, a thing that shines like a moon even though the night is completely dark, I run across rue Berri and I go through the broken doorway, I walk over the broken glass and whatever's lying on the floor even if it complains, I go to where the instruments are glowing in the darkness, on the second floor. The first sax I touch nestles into my hands as though it recognizes me.

That's why you won't find me beneath my sculpture in the Desjardins complex any more. I've left it to that miserable Louse, who is still playing his flute terribly. Me, I've moved west along Sainte-Catherine to the university, hidden by the crowd that surrounds me. With my arms extended I hold my sax, unless it's my sax that holds me. Someone inside me is playing, someone is playing so well that people all stop, even if they can't hear anything.

BABY

SINCE YOU met her, you go walking near her every week, and with every step you lose a little of your innocence.

The path towards her starts here, in this section of boulevard Mont-Royal that isn't yet called chemin de la Forêt. When you cross the invisible frontier between Montreal and Outremont, it's not a case of you leaving the city; the city retreats on tiptoe so as not to disturb the silent calm of wealth. Rustic cottages stare haughtily at the woods across the street. You always stop for a moment, trying for some insight into the people who live in those houses, trying to read the secret of their success in their expressions or the way they chew. There, more than anywhere else, you are attacked by envious thoughts, but that's another story. You cross boulevard Mont-Royal. The path into the woods still has the uneven appearance of a logging road. Here's what happens when you go into the woods: the envious thoughts trip over their own contradictions, the phantom of success is thrown beaten to the ground. Light and detached, in a mood of dangerous freedom, you advance.

This place is not overrun by people. Sometimes you know somebody's been by because of the dog shit on the path; dogs never come alone, without a human fastened to the other end of a leash. You look away when one of these couples appears in front of you, or you look at the dog. Some dogs manage to make you forget the unattractiveness of their masters.

Here, the squirrels flee domestication. In the winter, rabbit tracks make amusing patterns in the snow. Squadrons of crows, titmice, mynah birds, others whose names you don't know, flutter in the trees. So much for the visible beasts. But what reigns supreme here rises from the vegetal and the silence. You always feel out of place, a persistent virus contaminating a healthy body, but as the woods close about you, you strip off your factory-made skins and you recognize members of your essential family in these roots and trunks emerging from the soil. The evidence forces you to the welcome realization that you also come from this complex ground; so the needless questioning can stop now, you'd toss out your life like some disposable product if this conviction of your origins wasn't so precarious, so threatened with extinction when the city takes you up again.

In May the woods turn white, covered by anthrisci bearing flowers like umbrellas on their stems. Anthrisci are dense and abundant, though their existence is denied by most dictionaries. Their leaves, jagged like parsley, glow year round, and in the warm perfume they exhale are concealed suspect and narcotic properties. You know many things like that, things that have no social utility and that you are never able to slip into conversations.

The road towards her is filled with signs you haven't yet learned to decode. For example, farther along there are two maples lying dramatically close to the path, in an X or a cross, depending on the angle from which you come upon their enormous carcasses. They are tangled together in a way that might lead one to suspect a suicide, a crime of passion. One of these trees has a gaping wound at the base, so deep that strange animals must live there, barn owls or snowy owls, monsters of the night, reptiles that have been extinct for thousands of years. One day you examined the tree's heart with a pocket flashlight. You didn't find anything, you heard only the noise made by mythic beasts after they've escaped the world of reason.

There comes a time, on the path, when a wire fence reminds you that civilization is still nearby, lurking at your side. You go along the fence to the left, climbing over some knotgrass that twists beneath your feet. You step over a low barrier and now you're almost there. A cart of cut flowers is turned over in front of you, as though to welcome you. You know they're not meant for you, but you pick one up, a crimson carnation grotesquely tied with a fat bow.

Yes, you are in a cemetery. Cemeteries are like peaceful and neglected parks. In this one you can wander about, your eyes captivated by the yew trees, the oaks, the blooming peonies, the lilac bushes, you can choose to ignore anything mineral or frightening. The stones are discreet here, likewise their faded inscriptions. It could all be nothing more than a stage set.

Even the crematorium exudes the good will of a well-off household; you'd expect to see children and spaniels gambolling to the clink of cocktails and the laughter of young women. Until one day the doors were left open and you saw the nickel-plated ovens, sparkling with cleanliness and frequent use. After that you considered the building with a new respect.

Most of your deaths still lie ahead, in a future you know can be put off; you haven't yet been hit by the pain those nearest to you will cause, those you love, those who wish you no harm. But two or three of them are already slipping away from you, soon you'll see them go beyond the point of no return, and there's no armour strong enough, no place to keep the coming sorrows in order to tame them peacefully in advance.

Your first time here, you arrived with a tourist's candour, you read the inscriptions on the headstones the way you'd watch a movie's credits, you compared the tombstones and the calligraphy, you smiled at the quaint English surnames: Chiniquy, Proctor, Muckle, Pease, Dansken, Preby...Long dead, most of them buried in the last century, the reality of their existence dulled and improbable.

It wasn't until the next year that you met her. You were coming back from the hill at the cemetery's east, descending from the plateau that gives you a clear view of Montreal's greyness framed between its river and its skyscrapers. You were walking slowly. Otherwise you couldn't have noticed it, a marker timidly pounded into the earth, a poor-quality stone with a slightly blurred inscription. BABY, May 1947—January 1952.

Nothing more. No name, no sign of belonging to a line living or finished, this tiny mound and this succinct inscription on imitation granite. Just a rosebush. A rosebush that produces yellow flowers. You know that now.

It's the baby's youth that upset you, no doubt, the unjustified waste, it's the anonymity and the images of childhood that don't go with the heavy symbolism of bereavement. It's the precise moment when it ended: 1952.

That was a year you had to be alive, the world was a clay sculpture in the process of being shaped, Greek women won the right to vote, an airplane broke the sound barrier for the first time, East Germany put up an iron curtain against temptation, Hemingway hauled *The Old Man and the Sea* up from his oceanic depths, François Mauriac and Albert Schweitzer got the Nobel Prize, André Gide was placed on the index, the cinema spat out timeless masterpieces: *Forbidden Games, Golden Marie, Manon des Sources, The Quiet Man, High Noon...* And you, you came into the world, don't forget that, you came into the world in January convinced you were immortal.

That, above all, is the coincidence that upset you: are souls traded like cards, do some have to fall so others can emerge? You couldn't stop yourself from thinking that she left a space open for you that January, for you specifically.

Since then you come back to see Baby, every week you come to her, telling yourself she's expecting you, and admiring the splendid things the earth produces to be forgiven for taking us back.

You always think of her in the feminine, you know Baby is a little girl shrouded in non-being. It doesn't give you any macabre feelings, time gradually draws you into the woods, and the light is somehow dancing and eternal as you wind between the junipers and the beech trees of the Mont-Royal cemetery, and on the tiny marker you place the discarded flower you took from the crematorium, a carnation this time, you zigzag twice around the stone so she will recognize your step and join you. It's only afterwards, when you feel Baby's shadow behind you, that you start the Game.

It's a game you invented for her, to counter any sneak attacks of regret. You called it the Extrapolation Game. The rules are simple, just one helper is needed. The Player's age isn't important; that of the Helper, on the other hand, is fixed. The Player and the Helper must be alive; all other skills can be useful, but they are not indispensable. An imaginative Player paired with a distracted Helper make the best possible team; but here, as elsewhere, perfection is not necessary.

Your particular Helper is a woman of about forty, it doesn't matter which woman. The first part of the game consists of finding her, in the vastness of the cemetery, then following her discreetly and putting together deductions. The game is over when the Helper suddenly leaves the cemetery or when she turns around to give you dirty looks or swear at you. The Helpers don't know you're in the midst of playing with them: some get especially angry. The object of the game is to imagine, with the aid of the living Helpers, all the women—impassioned, faded or utterly confused—that Baby might have become.

The first woman you observed seemed a lot older than her age, forty-two, and moved about leadenly. Her clothes were poorly cut, the back of her raincoat was skewed to the left. Despite the clear sky she was carrying an umbrella under her arm. She wasn't just out for a walk, she knew where she was going and why and how long it would take her. There was no room in her for strolling, for the luxury of anything unnecessary. She didn't stop to smell the mock orange, although the branch was blocking her way and has a dizzying odour. Farther on, she took out a tissue and blew her nose roughly, tangled up in her umbrella, standing almost but not entirely still, as though annoyed by this sudden slowdown she hadn't planned. She carefully folded the used tissue in four and slid it into her right sleeve.

You weren't surprised to see her stop in the northern part of the cemetery, where there are just a few stunted trees, in front of a row of small matching stones decorated with plastic-coated yellow roses. A tiny duplex, in a clean suburban landscape. Her dead were Teriazos. She pulled her tissue from her sleeve and energetically rubbed the stone, as though to declare her ownership. She meticulously scraped the fallen leaves from the ground. And you clearly saw her reach out and then, sly and precise, take a flower from the neighbouring tombstone, her eyes shining like a child's.

You could easily imagine her children fighting, there are three of them, boys who devour anything edible, they're at that age, and watch television with the volume turned loud enough to stun. Sometimes there's a man beside her, late in the evening and on weekends, and he calls her "Baby," but "Baby" the way people say Maria or Teresa or "Pass me some more fish" and "Where's my shirt gone"? This Baby has a face stiffened by servitude and legs too thin for the fleshy body they're forced to support, but they go, they walk themselves to exhaustion in every direction, her legs circle the globe ten times a year even if they've never gone back to Greece. You can also hear the howling inside her, a grief that grows old because it's never allowed out, that in its silence smothers everything that was alive and joyous back then, it's been so long, back then.

That time you stopped the game before your Helper, and you were the first to leave the cemetery.

Another day, the weather was very beautiful, you followed a young woman who was forty-two but looked thirty, you had to be very close to see the mutinous way her skin was beginning to wither around her eyes. She was strolling along with a man who kept giving her troubled looks, which after a brief delay she would return, her hand loyally in his but her face inattentive. This woman's clothes hung on her like a second skin; you noticed the perfect curved motions of her body as she walked. They didn't go far, up to the birch tree that looks over one of the crossroads. It was a good place to pause, or to act out a slow improvisation: they realized this at once and took out blankets to sit on, cold cuts and bottles.

The woman didn't sit down immediately, she moved around the tree in the sun and the shade, searching for the right spot, she wanted just the right light for her tan. Finally she allowed her neck the sun, kept her face protected but her legs also in the sun—a difficult position she forced herself to maintain for some time. While he cut the bread, she slid her blouse a bit down her shoulder, then changed her mind and undid a few buttons instead, down where yellow roses crossed prettily over her belly. And all during lunch, while he murmured love talk to her, Baby, oh Baby, you saw her quivering like a squirrel as she pushed a curl back into place or checked her eye make-up, nibbled at a few pieces of fruit, refused fattening bread, studied the shape of her hands and the way they lay on each other.

This Baby is so transparent, a woman who will never know how to pass through mirrors, you can see she's paralysed by her reflection, which she watches with a terrifying anxiety, little Alice helpless against passing time and deepening wrinkles, you see her chasing after her youth with everything from jogging to massage to cosmetic surgery. Since she discovered she is no longer twenty years old she has stopped celebrating her birthday, when she runs she watches the vulture above her head, she runs with a cucumber cream mask on her face and skin softener around her eyes. Every day is one day less of triumphant youth, every second added is a curse, every night a prayer that science or God will find a cure to mummify her body, to keep it alive and firm through all eternity.

The final Baby was very different, coming from a contemporary and motorized species that left you admiring and incredulous for several minutes. You heard her before you saw her, you were looking for her around the corners of the paths, and then suddenly a purring Mercedes set her down in front of you. She leapt from the car with a determined laugh and a yellow rose in her lapel, she was dressed casually in a modest suit that didn't try to disguise her forty-two years, most of all she was filled with amazing energy. Two men, obviously subordinates, followed her; she showed them the tombs and the headstones with a businesswoman's gestures and they took notes. She didn't pace the ground like some necrophiliac tourist. Every pebble she stepped on seemed to clink like a coin. You never knew what she did, but you knew she did it very well.

Her voice was that of a woman familiar with life and with power, who remembers the daunting height of every rung of the ladder she's had to climb. Her sentences didn't trail off into those questioning inflections women often use to seek approval. She was saying: you will take this down for me, you will measure that for me, how much do you think that, and the men were obeying promptly, they were showing her the same respect they would have shown to one of their own, exactly the same, no added weight of flirtation or seduction.

She didn't stay long, she had a lot to do, an engineering survey somewhere in Toronto, that's what she said suddenly, looking at her digital watch. Her preoccupied eyes passed over you, a negligible quantity, as she climbed back into her car. The engine had been running the whole time.

You like that one, she has aperitifs in the bars of good hotels, she eats sushi while watching the sun set over European capitals, she has lovers who are sometimes younger than her, sometimes older, her mind has not been moulded by obedience, life is always offering her attractive detours. Just the same, look how the details of her existence are still imperfect, look at her at night when she's unable to sleep in her luxurious suite, in Bangkok or Montreal, look at her swallowing sleeping pills and tranquilizers. She's been having the same nightmare for months, the word "Baby" appears from nowhere and plunges her into blackness, she dreams of the children she didn't have, she sees them playing every night in sunlit parks from which she is excluded, the idiotic routine she didn't want—cajoling, scolding, putting a band-aid on the hurt, picking up the fallen teddy bear—whirls about her laughing at her sterile career, and she wakes up every morning with the terrible conviction that she's been cheated.

You could also talk about others, the one who weeds the mortuary plot as though it were a garden, the one who sings softly, the one who wears extravagant hats, the one who cries in front of her father's tomb...Some days, the Helpers escape in all directions and the Extrapolation Game becomes difficult to play. Behind you, you hear Baby's shadow getting tired, you press her with questions: Would you have liked to be this one?… Do you like that one better?… There are so many of them, the potential Babys, they are all so different. Why does every one of them have that hidden nameless anxiety, that sly mouse gnawing at their entrails.

Every time the Game ends and you're getting ready to pass through the cemetery's gothic gateway, you hear Baby's happy sigh as she goes back to her non-existent five-year-old self, you hear her relief as she rejoins the mound beneath the yellow rosebush. Death is nothing, she assures you. Compared to that, it's nothing.

PINK AND WHITE

FOR *Marco Micone*

DON'T LOOK for the signature, there isn't one. You can't put a face or a throwaway envelope to the words I'm writing you; that way they go one by one into your heart, as impossible to erase as perfume. Ugo Lagorio, I am one of your students, and for the moment that's all. Twice a week you teach me the language of our common ancestors, and I learn it the same way you teach, devoid of nostalgia, the way you polish old jewels. Twice a week, that's not very much and yet it's enough to keep me absolutely sure of the first true conviction I've ever had: I am the love of your life, Ugo Lagorio, and neither of us can do anything about it.

I know you as much more than the man who teaches Italian for money, classes you throw yourself into even though they bore you to death, I've memorized all of your books, even the driest essays, and I hide in the sparse audiences of the public lectures you give. Don't make the mistake of misunderstanding me, *professore*, I'm not some fanatic idiotic groupie who goes wet hearing your words. I'm a young, intelligent person stunned to come against a sister intelligence, stunned to recognize my thoughts in your words, thoughts I had before you expressed them.

Like you, I've had enough of being an immigrant. Like you, I rail against those who snuggle into their immigrant status the way they would into an incurable disease. My parents have been speaking English to me ever since I was born,

English and Italian to keep me where I am, clinging to our Saint-Léonard families and the American dream, my parents would like me to spend my whole life on my knees before the votive light of a country whose time is past. I was born here, I'm not an immigrant, I want to make this land mine. Since I've realized this place is French-speaking, I refuse to cut myself off from the dominant majority, I refuse to stagnate in the ranks of the excluded, I refuse to speak English with my parents. War has broken out between us, they curse me with the same words our hostile community uses against you and your traitorous freedom, *racist traitor traditrice*, and I must get away from them to learn how to fight this ridiculous battle, alone but accompanied by your books, which keep my resolve firm.

Ugo Lagorio, I too write. Just hesitant attempts now, content to gradually strip down the language in order to find the centre, but soon I'll be writing novels, and I'll be better than the best writers here, I'll be more Francophone than those who've lived here for ever and much more determined than them to master the language until it curls up at my feet.

It's not arrogance that makes me speak this way, it's the fighting genes of the new arrival that are still spinning about inside me, inside us, *professore*, for neither you nor I are yet accepted in this so-vulnerable country, you know it more painfully than I, how many times have I heard you publicly describe the reasons you migrated here, how many times will we be asked to justify our existence, how many more times?

What awaits us, both of us, is a fate that could be exhilarating: never melting into the stultifying homogeneity, being condemned to live with the rough edges of our intimate parts, which refuse to shape themselves to fit the puzzle.

Ugo Lagorio, we are mutants.

That is the word for your pain, for our pain.

There are times when, without warning, what I am forced to call my "Italianness" surges forth like a gust of heat I'd like to be able to kick out the door. I don't know what this annoying ghost wants from me—I've never gone to Italy, I've always hated pasta, I don't know what part of my brain it keeps haunting but the more I deny its existence, the more it digs into me and hurts me.

You see, there's nothing like a mutant to understand another mutant's pain.

It's not that your wife doesn't try her best; on the contrary. It's not for lack of intelligence or beauty that she can't understand you. I've seen her with you, I've seen how impossible it is for her to do anything for you. You have to admit the obvious, she was born here and women born here are as cold and bitter as winter apples, beautiful but cold and sour, so far removed from the joyous ghost that sings inside you, even if you do your best to exorcize it.

I have never liked apples. Our fruit is figs—don't laugh, Ugo Lagorio—figs that split in the sun, figs whose juice is sweeter than Canadian pastries, it's not our fault if we have the memory of figs in our blood, and a need for passion that is dying of cold, but survives.

I'm sure you don't make love with her any more.

Love.

Ugo, Ugo Lagorio, I repeat your name and fire spreads through my insides, fire squirts out of me and illuminates whatever I touch, borders sorrows tensions snowbanks melt from afar and become sacred lakes on which I dance.

That is love, the love I'm offering you and preparing to take from you, because I am taking you, I'm uprooting you from your loveless life, I am beautiful, don't worry, I am so beautiful that when your eyes pick me out from the forty-five faces of the class they blink, and I am not some timid virgin

Italian woman, all my doors are open to you, they won't trap you in ambush, with me you'll be in a state of dangerous freedom, I will give wings to your deepest desires. My father was born in the same village as you, that can't be a coincidence, but my father has nothing to do with you, don't think I'm looking for my father in you, I'm an eighteen-year-old woman, a Quebecker without a past, I'm a woman and I forbid you to find me too young. There's no age for being young, and anyway you're much more so than I, Ugo Lagorio.

I'll slide this letter into your box without being seen and then I'll wait a bit before letting you recognize me, I'll wait until these words—these velvet-coated claws—have sunk in and prepared my way, I won't wait long.

We'll take our first trip together this spring, it won't matter where we go, in the Far North or even in Italy we'll make all our hotel rooms sizzle.

Watch out, Ugo Lagorio, I'm coming to kill the half-lived life that's killing you.

CHILD'S PLAY

FOUR FORTY-FIVE in the afternoon. Marie has her
thumb out, her bag is wedged between her ankles like a shapeless beast. The weather is muggy, the trees in the Parc
Lafontaine are edged purple in the dusk.

Four forty-eight. A white Renault 5 stops in front of Marie.
The driver leans out, he has Ronald Reagan's ravaged eyes and
a well-worn trenchcoat.

"Where are you going?" he inquires.

"Where are you going yourself?" Marie replies.

Four fifty-two. The white Renault 5 is creeping along.
Over her crossed legs Marie's skirt is a small dark brazen stroke
with nothing to hide. The driver's eyes waver towards it.

"What's your name?" He pretends to be interested.

"Twenty bucks," Marie says. "No penetration. Twenty-five
for a blow job, five more if you touch."

It makes her smile every time, she can't help thinking of
leeks or strawberries: it's three dollars for one box, twenty-five
if you take a dozen. But the driver doesn't smile. He has turned
red, gotten upset, there's not enough space in his nose for him
to breathe. The silence lasts a block.

"Where?" He suddenly gives up.

"Here."

"In the car?"

Yes. She knows the city, its empty nooks and crannies,
there's a quiet alleyway nearby just asking to be used. As for
the Renault 5 seats, they're famous for reclining fully.

Five-oh-eight. The white Renault 5, its doors locked, is

parked at the side of a nameless blind alley. The driver's pants have been pulled down to his thighs. The driver's body, collapsed in the shape of a capital I on the reclined seat, quivers, shakes and shudders. The driver's penis is in Marie's mouth. It's a little one, and already seems about to explode, but doesn't. Before stretching out, the driver put an environmental music tape into his stereo. Now all sorts of lapping sounds can be heard in the car, adorned every now and then by the small cries of surprised birds. The driver has closed his eyes, he moans a bit, he must think he's lying in a mossy clearing in the shadow of a gurgling waterfall. As for Marie, she is twisting about, annoyed because all this water going glubglubglub makes her need to pee. There are also loud rumblings from the driver's stomach. Marie thinks of the coloured illustrations of digestion she saw recently in a book, the small and large intestines, the jejunum and the ileum, she has to force herself not to burst out laughing, she has always had a tendency to giggle at the wrong time.

Five-twenty. The driver ejaculates into Marie's mouth. Marie thinks of cold pure milk, of cream soda, of the foamy vanilla milkshakes of her early childhood, she thinks about other things, but it isn't easy.

Five twenty-two. The driver is crying. They often cry that way, after. Marie doesn't worry about it and waits calmly. Just liquids, lost for ever. Without looking at her the driver gives her everything he's got in his wallet, which is forty-two dollars. He asks her if he can drop her off somewhere.

Five thirty-three. Marie is on the escalator in The Bay, she goes to the fourth floor. The people around her seem tired and sullen; it's because of their work, or the time, or the neon lights, or all of it together.

Five thirty-seven. Marie goes back down The Bay's escalator, her bag under one arm, a big parcel in the other.

Five fifty-seven. Marie goes home. She eats sausages and mashed potatoes.

Six thirty-four. Marie is sitting on her bed. She opens her bag, takes out her geography and math books, pushes them into a corner. She unwraps the parcel. It's a white bear cub, plush, with a black nose and gleaming eyes. Marie takes the bear cub, lies down with it, cuddles into its synthetic heat, stays like that for hours, a vague smile on her lips. When you're twelve, something like that can still make you happy.

LEAH AND PAUL, FOR EXAMPLE

February 1991. Afternoon.

There were the sheets, the pink and mauve towels, the pile of embroidered tablecloths, the green-apple bath oil, the Scandinavian dinnerware, the fluted champagne glasses, the genuine clay casserole dishes. Now it's all over, split in two as though hacked by a maniac cleaver; the apartment is like an oilfield ripe for speculators. Now they are in the kitchen. She has opened a cupboard. He is following each of her actions as though through a magnifying glass, like a disbelieving detective.

"Surely we're not going to divide the herbs."

"I'm taking them."

Which is what she does. The sage, fennel, basil, all the jars he has taken the trouble to label in Letraset on silvered vinyl are balanced precariously in her arms. He doesn't protest immediately, for the sake of the jars he waits until she has deigned to put them down somewhere, she has always been a bit slow.

"There's no way you're taking all that."

"They're MY herbs. It's always been me who takes care of them."

"I'm the one who dried them. The jars are mine!"

"Fine. I'll put them into plastic bags."

"I don't have any plastic bags."

Bastard. Fucking bastard. She turns the words over in her mind, touches them from inside, they have a texture, a smoothness that would make them so satisfying to spit out.

She keeps quiet for the moment.

"I'll bring the jars back later," she says.

"No. At least leave me the basil. The basil and the tarragon."

"You know they're the ones I like best!"

"Okay. I'll keep the fennel. And the basil."

"Why the basil? I'm not leaving you the basil."

The light surprises them from the side and forces them to blink. Their faces seem dragged down by something acrid and purulent, hate makes them tremble like crippled animals.

August 1988. Evening.

He touches her arm. Lightly, with the fat part of his thumb, a spider's touch she could let pass without noticing. She responds to him immediately, she has radar sleeping beneath her skin which wakes only when he makes contact—that's what she often tells him, anyway, with a big throaty laugh so it doesn't sound too soft-hearted. He increases the pressure on her arm. Beneath the tissue he can sense the stammer of an infinitely disturbing heat, he slides his fingers along her collarbone and comes to rest at the tips of her breasts, that part of her which electrifies both of them. She always wears her breasts like jewels, provocative and erect at the slightest excuse. It might seem her smile is for herself, she lets the scissors, the sprigs of parsley, the thyme, the marjoram fall to the grass, she takes off her sweater. He goes for her breasts right away, his hands hurry to knead her, to force her sharp wild cries. She looks him in the eyes, then reaches down to his zipper, she rubs his crotch and goes right to the place where it's swollen and warm, then caresses his sex admiringly, as though running her fingers along velvet.

They collapse to their knees, felled by a surge that is beyond them, into the dizzying odours of basil, tarragon, they tear off their clothes. She's so wet and writhing that her vulva keeps slipping in and out of his fingers, she swallows his sex up to the hilt, they are everywhere and nowhere, struggling nobly to ensure that life will never leave them.

"Wait," she says suddenly.

She holds him off for several seconds, yes, it's infinitely good, this moment before orgasm is worth stretching out, extreme tension, the frenzy of desire that rattles every particle of the body, we will never be more alive, more intense, always remember this. He comes in her from behind, she's the first to explode and their cries roll through the darkness to the cores of the stars.

March 1990. Night.

Through the window, above Mont Royal, she sees a star quivering. Perhaps it's Vega or the North Star, she can't be sure, the sky is diluted by the city lights. She looks away, just across from the bed, for example. On the wall is a silkscreen print, a serene seascape from which she sees, in the darkness, just a hint of light. She no longer knows where to look for reassurance; at night the familiar world slips away, cannot be counted on.

She is waiting for him. She keeps herself from thinking that she is waiting for him, instead she tells herself she has insomnia. He must have run into someone, an old pal he hasn't seen since he was a teenager, in their euphoria they will have eaten together, had two three four liqueurs, he just forgot to phone, these things happen. Or a car. She sees a long red car coming out of an intersection, she tries to make herself think about something else but the car calmly drives into her head and then, swift and gleaming, carries out various complicated manoeuvres before crashing into him, he who always crosses the street without looking. She closes her eyes, she's unable to shake these images of crushed bodies emptying their blood into hospital corridors, she'll never get back to sleep. It's three o'clock in the morning.

The telephone rings. Her hands go right to the receiver. She waits.

"It's me," he says.

It's him. He's alive. He doesn't sound drunk. In the end there's a rational explanation for everything.

"Weren't you asleep yet?"

His voice trembles, the way it does when he's uneasy. She knows his voice by heart. Suddenly, her worry about him dying gives way to another worry, infinitely more complex.

"Listen," he says. "Listen…" He blurts it all out at once, for fear of being interrupted or losing his place in the speech he's rehearsed—"I'm not coming home tonight, I don't feel like coming home, don't get upset, we've already talked about it, it's nothing serious, it's just one night, go to sleep, it's nothing."

It's true they have already talked about it. These things happen. Above all, never lie, don't live in fear of a little incidental lust. We're all adults. Occasional straying can make a couple stronger.

She goes back to bed and curls up in a ball. She feels stunned, numb. To tame the howling demons, she keeps repeating to herself, over and over, it's nothing, go to sleep, it's nothing, nothing.

November 1989. Late afternoon.

He has bought flowers. Heather, Chinese lilies, mimosa, a couple of red anthuriums; he is very proud of the irregular harmony they make in the centre of the table. He has put the bottle of vintage Roederer in the refrigerator, beside the scallop conserve and the lobsters. Nothing is too beautiful, some days, when his heart gurgles with joy and he sees indigo in even the blackest cloud.

But there's no special occasion, no spectacular event to celebrate, nothing that wasn't already there in the daily routine. It came over him this afternoon at work, he started thinking about her, about them. Especially the other one, who was galloping towards them, splitting apart the universe: theoretically they hadn't wanted any, they hadn't done it on purpose. That's how children happen most of the time, when people are in their usual state of inattention. At the beginning he concealed his hesitation, he accepted the fact that she accepted it. The feedings, the inevitable squalling, the unavoidable overwork and exhaustion, the disrupted intimacy, their whole life to be reconstructed from the bottom up, the idiocies to be recommenced by proxy, Father Stork watching horrified over his brat's escapades; it was enough to keep him from sleeping. Then he got used to the idea. Today, for almost no reason at all, a little kid swearing loudly as he walked under his window, the wonderful news struck home, he became wildly and appallingly happy about his future paternity.

Lovesick, he waits for her; patiently and laughing all alone he waits for THEM. On a candlelit evening when he's an old man, his daughter will tell him naughty interplanetary stories, and in a stentorian voice his son will sing computer hymns.

He hears her coming. She opens the door, she seems amazed to find him there. She sees the flowers. She walks up to him, frail and limping, she takes his two hands.

"I just had an abortion," she murmurs.

He finds nothing to say. She seems overcome by such great pain that there is nothing to say.

"Suddenly I was afraid," she says. "I'm afraid of children."

She presses against him, inundated by an immense fatigue. Giving something up has never been so cruel, but in the end, surrounded by his warmth, she grows calm, he rocks her in his arms for hours, sobbing to himself like an imbecile.

April 1987. Morning.
She is tall for a woman. It should be said that she stands very straight, with a hint of arrogance, and she looks at him without blinking, as one does while sizing up an opponent.

"I want unemployment insurance," she says.

"Of course. Why not?"

He is sitting behind a desk that doesn't seem to match him: some files, aseptic plants, a small glaring light that's very twentieth-century Inquisition. He's wearing a soft flannel shirt, and the corners of his mouth are turned up in a way that makes it seem he's laughing inside every time he speaks.

"How much would you like?" he asks.

"Uh…the maximum, obviously."

"Obviously."

He begins to fill out a form. She watches him as he works, his brow slightly wrinkled.

"What are you writing?"

"The usual things. You should get your first cheque within a few weeks."

"Aren't you supposed to ask me a bunch of questions first?"

"That's right." He excuses himself and stops writing. "What would you like me to ask you?"

She starts to laugh; he tries to keep a straight face but, as already noted, the corners of his mouth keep lifting.

"I don't know." She smiles. "Why I left my job. What time I get up. How many thousand CVs I've sent out and to whom and prove it."

"All right. What time do you get up?"

"Very early. Not to look for work but because I have insomnia."

"Well. Me too."

"You're not much of a bureaucrat," she notes mildly.

"I know," he admits. "I handed in my resignation today."

"Is that true?"

"It's true."

He closes the file, he has finished writing. She should get up, but she doesn't right away.

"I'm having dinner at the Funambule," she suggests.

"Okay. Me too."

"My name is Leah."

"I know. It's written in your file. I'm Paul."

"I know. It's written on your desk."

They look at each other, they smile at each other, very satisfied with themselves and the turn the day is taking.

May 1988. Late afternoon.

The old Renault coughs, hacks, stops. They exchange a tragic look.

"Oh Christ," he says, upset.

"Yeah," she sighs.

They have broken down a few kilometres from Anavissos. They are surrounded by cypress trees, climbing pistachios, the odours of eucalyptus and wild olive trees, a dry and pleasantly savage beauty but nothing much like—or in any way like— a garage. They could stop a passing car, but no cars are passing, which seemed the height of perfection a few minutes ago. With nothing else to do, they start walking. They are on what's called the Apollonian coast, the ocean splashing in their face as though they were on a postcard. Suddenly a peasant in his field, beside his donkey and a hundred tomato plants. She runs towards him. With Socratic impassivity the peasant watches her throw herself at him. She brings out her Sunday Greek.

"*Kalimera*," she begins, "can you tell me, *boreite na mou deite...*"

She returns, very proud, with a rusty Vespa. The peasant has agreed to rent it to her for a few hours in exchange for an astronomical sum plus all her credit cards as a guarantee—alas, the simple, unsophisticated rustic is a species threatened with extinction. But never mind, it's still not impossible for them to make Cape Sounion before twilight. She is absolutely determined to see the sixteen Doric columns of Poseidon's temple aflame in the rays of the setting sun—she has read fantastic descriptions of this phenomenon.

They jolt along the winding road. With every bump they howl in pain; the Vespa is endowed with all the suspension and braking power of a swallow's turd in free fall. Suddenly they spot the celebrated columns perched on the celebrated promontory. White lace, vulnerable and eternal, looking out to sea. It leaves them breathless.

They climb up to the marble terrace. The site is astoundingly beautiful and, above all, totally deserted: just cats, cats all over the place, and a dozing guard who sells them two tickets. They sit amidst the poppies, above the Gulf of Saronica, beside the white temple. Gripped by Homeric bliss, they wait for the sun to set. He inspects the sky.

"Looks like black clouds, there..."

"No," she says decisively, "in Greece it never rains."

At a quarter after five, twenty-two buses appear on the highway and, in less time than it takes to say it, they vomit a million Germans onto the white marble. The Germans wave, they call to each other, they take pictures, they jump around on the sacred stones, they are obviously waiting for the setting sun to set fire to the sixteen columns of Poseidon's temple. To avoid being trampled, Leah and Paul move aside. At twenty-five minutes after five a torrential rain begins.

They climb back onto their Vespa, so choking with laughter that even the cats, seeing them pass, condescend to give them an amused wink.

December 1989. Night.
Of course, it began with something insignificant. Even world wars spring, it's said, from something insignificant. A fateful supper, at her family's. He laughed, that was his mistake. He laughed at an untoward joke—in her opinion nasty—that someone made about her. She is wounded, she feels betrayed by him. He blames the alcohol—and what about politeness, I kill myself trying to be civilized with your family. She as much as calls him a coward. That he does not accept. He swells up, like the frog in the fable. They belabour each other with their families as though they were shameful diseases, they blurt out spiteful words that they're a thousand miles from believing.

And now they're lying side by side as though they were in a huge frozen dormitory. They are sulking. Everything would be so easy if one of them would admit to being vulnerable; I was wrong, forgive me. But they are trapped in their pride; for the first time they are refusing to give ground—and besides, they've forgotten what started it. All that's left is an undefined rancour that leaves them gasping, and a terrible feeling of being alone.

He is the first to make an opening move: he puts his hand on her back. She is instantly relieved and grateful, she is dying to roll against him, but inside a small voice sneers: it's easy, it's really too easy, and she becomes stiff and hostile again. He doesn't insist.

He goes to sleep. Bitterly she watches him sleep—why didn't he persevere? What is this egotistical calm that takes him so far away from her?—she watches him sleeping the way we watch the sinking of the boat containing all our hopes.

July 1990. Noon.

He sees her—she is standing between two cars, carrying on some sort of argument. He finds this funny because neither one of them is where they're supposed to be: he ought to be working at the chalet, and officially she is imprisoned on location, filming. As always, interesting things happen by chance. He waves his arms at her, is about to call out her name. That's when he sees the blond guy. The blond guy was there before, he's the one she was arguing with, but now she's leaning forward, now she's kissing him, now she's suddenly making him blindingly real.

They walk together on the sidewalk, a meaningless stroll except for the motion of his hand on her upper arm. Far behind, he follows, he can't take his eyes off that hand, their matching stride, the shoulders that keep bumping into each other. They go into a restaurant. This time, he saw it clearly, she leaned against him in the entrance, an instinctive thrusting of her chest against him before she brushed his lips with hers, he would swear it, their heads are concealed by a partition but he imagines them moving towards each other in slow motion, and this fictional vision is more unbearable than the rest.

He has positioned himself on the other side of the street, like in a bad thriller, astounded to find himself the third party in an ordinary affair. He doesn't have a pistol in his pocket, just an old shrivelled wallet to knead in his distress. A fat woman bumps into him without stopping. "Excuse me, sir," he murmurs, he no longer knows what he's saying, or what he's doing there, taking root in the sidewalk, or how much of all this he's making up. He leaves.

Later he calls her. He pretends to be talking to her from a telephone booth far away in the Laurentians. Her voice is cool and candid, he feels reality blurring, becoming comfortable again. He asks her how the filming is going. She's got too much to do, she says, another insane day—not even time to eat. She keeps talking but he doesn't hear any more, he is wondering, amazed, where this weird pain cutting him in two is coming from.

October 1987. Evening.
It's a great party. The guests munch, drink, chatter, snort high-quality coke, smoke Quebec and Colombian grass, dance in perfectly unrestrained ecstasy. These are all the right people, they seem to have been poured from a single set of moulds. It was her idea, an irrepressible desire to celebrate, a way of saying: look, here's my past and my parallel lives, do you still want me? They have brought together their respective friends, their old lovers, their faded loves, in fact, without telling anyone, they are celebrating the beginning of an eternal epoch, the Leah-Paul cohabitation.

They flit from one guest to the next, reveal themselves as impeccable hosts. The evening advances and they only have time to brush against each other in passing, a faraway wink across the room, an impromptu kiss on the neck. But through the others and the distance that separates them they can feel their extreme complicity, their unwavering magnetic attraction, like an animal feigning sleep.

She is in full flight when he suddenly grabs her and whispers, "I want to talk to you, come here for a few minutes." His tone is emphatic, she pretends to be worried. They look through the crowded apartment for a quiet corner, they end up among the coats in the vestibule.

"Here it is," he says, "a surprise, a present for you."

He holds out something white, Keith Jarrett's *The Köln Concert* album. She starts to laugh so hard that she chokes.

"What is it?" he asks, annoyed.

She holds them, him and the album, tightly against her, she nibbles traitorously at his nose.

"I bought the same thing for you."

The evening continues and people begin to wonder where they are. Someone comes across them unexpectedly and goes back to broadcast the news to the others, with nostalgic indulgence. They are lying down in the midst of the coats, burrowed into kilometres of raingear, kissing and hugging as though they were all alone in the world.

January 1991. Evening.
The knives are flying. They are equally skilled in this cruel little game that consists of firing poisoned arrows at each other's most vulnerable spots, and they aren't holding back. It must have been ripe to burst, but the abscess isn't draining, they are up to their necks in the purulence and bad faith of a dying grand passion. Liar, you lied to me, he screams, it's your fault, you pushed me to the limit, she spits back, they've forgotten that words are anything but rocks to be thrown in each other's faces. They go over their life together scene by scene and they dissect it until it's unrecognizable—there, and there, look what you did to me, but remember that and that, you sneaky ingrate low-down con artist bitch.

The accusations pile up and neutralize each other, oh how can I get to you and hurt you as much as I myself am hurt? They pass from words to deeds. She breaks a flowerpot, throws the pieces in his face. He shakes her and pushes her violently against the wall. And then they stop, halt, silence, cut.

They stare at each other, frightened, in an end-of-the-world silence. What have we done, what have you done with your heart, where did it go?

They begin to blubber, each as ridiculous as the other. They are blubbering because of these few steps too close to the irreparable, they blubber because it's snowing outside, because it's a new year and they can't even find consolation in each other's arms.

June 1992. Evening.
The theatre empties quietly. Near the exit they suddenly find themselves face to face: impossible to pretend distraction or convenient myopia. It was bound to happen one day. He's with a girl, a tall, stylish redhead who's holding him victoriously by the elbow. She is alone.

For a moment they stand there bewildered, incapable of mastering the surprise and consternation spreading across their faces. Then they begin returning to normal, gradually finding the comfortable words that pass for communication.

"How's it going?"

"Well. And you?"

Fortunately, after a brief improvisation on the weather, they have the film to talk about. She notices that his eyes are shadowed, he is working too hard or maybe the tall redhead is lasciviously consuming his nights. She doesn't really want to know. He notices that she is faintly rounded, as though the sharpest angles have been smoothed out, perhaps she's pregnant. He doesn't really want to find out. They talk long enough to save face. The tall redhead casually eyes the exit.

They say goodbye, using the same words as those who have never loved each other.

Nonetheless, they were on the verge of really talking to each other when the crowd pushed them together, but the moment passed, there are too many spectators and the play is over. They leave and go off in opposite directions. They don't turn back, no confused looks across the emptiness, they leave very quickly, carried on the wings of fear.

September 1989. Night.

She's the one who keeps the fire, like the vestals of ancient times. Knowingly she intersperses the damp birch with the cherrywood logs, she keeps the air moving through with her magic wand, she tops it all off with a big armful of red pine that sends the flames leaping towards the sky.

"It's hell," he says, pulling back his chair.

The night is redolent of resin and the lake. They don't speak. As soon as they're out of Montreal and into this place, the wild heart of their forest, they become someone else, a new species, half animal, half human, welcomed into the grand movements of the cosmos. A raccoon has come to visit them. Before that two skunks, crafty and lame, snuck between their legs to steal potato chips. In the old spruce tree across from them, three flying squirrels have been performing reckless aerial leaps, just for them. It's endless, the actors play on and on, and they didn't even have to buy a ticket.

Now it's the moon. Red-tinged, almost round, it emerges from behind the mountain and hangs above the water.

"Come on," he whispers, "let's go out in the canoe."

They slip into the boat, glide along Indian-style, the water silent on their paddles. In front of them the moon traces a phosphorescent path; if they take it to the end they'll lose themselves in the stars, drown what's left of their fears, pierce the enigmas of the universe the way you prick a balloon. Suddenly the call of a loon. They stop in the middle of the lake.

It's a plaintive cry, a psalm, a supernatural chant. They are there in the midst of all that, the fire dancing on the shore, the moon, the night-calm lake, the song of the loon, their fingers find each other without looking, they wish they could cry— this love is such a state of grace, it's impossible that it won't last forever.

WOMEN HAVE MORE CLASS THAN MEN

HE KNOWS she's called Mirella because the first time he saw her she was unlocking the door of her apartment in the company of a girl who was saying, "He's killing me, Mirella, I swear he's killing me." Then, another time, they ran into each other in the stairway, he encumbered by bags of groceries that came up to his chin, she encumbered by nothing on her brown legs that came up to her waist, and he greeted her, smiling over the leeks and radish leaves, but she must not have heard him because she didn't reply.

And now this girl who is called Mirella and whom he finds attractive is almost naked beside him.

To tell the truth, they are separated by the balcony divider, along with many other things, but he's bathing in the emanations of her suntan lotion, and if he raised his eyes from his computer perhaps he would be tanned by the ultraviolet rays bombarding her. He doesn't raise his eyes from his computer. He mustn't look. She is gradually taking off her minimal outfit, one side of her brassiere falls down when she anoints herself with the sacrificial oil, an entire buttock makes its entrance into the free air, but above all he mustn't look. Women have the right to undress for themselves alone, for the sun, to combat osteoporosis, women don't like feeling exposed even when they expose themselves. Keeping his head down and his restless eyes on the screen makes him so tense that he jerks and knocks down his parasol, which obliges him to lean over and retrieve it, his eyes thus moving to her; and it's at this exact moment, brief, unique, that she chooses to turn towards him, to note that he is looking at her, and eye him scornfully and offendedly before covering herself in her peignoir and disappearing inside.

His name is Thomas, he is thirty-nine and is slowly getting over a difficult separation. He writes film scripts that he is able to sell after multiple revisions and compromises. He has experience with all sorts of compromise. The script he's working on tells the story of a transsexual, a man who has chosen to live in the body of a woman—or, to be exact, a man who is convinced that he is a woman whom nature swindled out of her body, and who is determined to reconquer it. A complicated and impossible story, and he no longer knows how he'll resolve it or why he began it.

The sun falls swiftly on the trees in the park, humidity begins to float like incense through the air, he is still sitting on the balcony. He sees musicians beating their tom-toms near the Victory statue, he sees a man urinating into a grove, a slender girl dancing. He sees couples, children, dogs, food being spread out on picnic tables. He sees humanity divided into two opposing and irreducible camps: on one hand the Warriors, who piss in the groves, on the other the Bacchanalians, who dance to the sound of the drums.

How might they get together?

When he's in the kitchen to make himself a quick salad he hears women's voices from Mirella's balcony. The one who said, "He's killing me," is now saying, "I swear, a bull in a china shop," and they laugh like teenagers, twisted by cascades of pleasure that leave them gasping. His nostrils are tickled by the odour of the grass they're smoking and he's suddenly cast back to the old days, the days when happiness could be found everywhere, in smoke and in laughter. Without looking for an excuse he goes out onto the balcony. There are three of them, including Mirella, who is wearing a red dress. When they see him they stop. He says good evening to them. "Good evening," Mirella replies, but not the others, and suddenly they're swept by an enormous tide of laughter that puts a wall up around them and hints that he should disappear inside.

During the evening his wife telephones. His ex-wife, though he doesn't like thinking of her that way. She asks him some perfunctory questions about his health, then gets to the heart of the matter. "He's not back yet," she says.

He being John, he for whom two years ago she threw so many things overboard, including Thomas.

Her voice is so low and depressed that he has to make an effort to hear: "He never calls to say he won't be coming. Here I am, like some cow, waiting for him. I could go to a café too, sit out and have a drink with some friends, instead of waiting for him." She sighs, he imagines her swaying near the telephone, a lock of tortured hair between her teeth. "Why doesn't he call? That's all I ask of him, to let me know when he isn't coming. I'm just asking for a bit of respect. Is that too much to ask?... A woman would never be like that, did any woman ever do that to you?" He bites his lip to stop from replying right away, God knows what might come out if he let himself speak freely, but fortunately it's not a real question. "One thing's for sure," she immediately adds with a bitter laugh, "it'll never change, women have more class than men."

He hears a noise behind her, she moves away for a moment, then comes back, transformed, animated, warm. "He's here," she says. *"The fucking bastard."* Then she gives a real laugh, filled with joyous relief. She doesn't ask him about his script. She invites him to dinner Saturday. "I'll make osso buco, you used to love my osso buco." He says he doesn't know, he doesn't think he can.

Afterwards, gripped by a terrible anger, he's unable to work. He goes out on the rail. He sees a red dress leaning against the balcony but he chooses to ignore it, to act as though he were alone, as though he were the only human being on earth contemplating the trees in the park as they give way to the shadows. She's the one to speak. She asks him for a match. He has one, even though he doesn't smoke. She lights a cigarette, incendiary in her red robe. And then she is asking him questions, what he does, where he lived before, and she listens to his answers looking straight ahead, her brow lightly furrowed. From her dark hair comes the smell of caramel, her mouth without lipstick is as red as her dress. How can he resist the desire to penetrate further into the disturbing intimacy of this odour, of all this red? He tells her he has a bottle of Sauterne in the refrigerator, he offers her a drink. She looks directly at him for the first time, glimmers of mauve flash from her eyes and she says, "Certainly not."

He works late into the night. This man-woman to whom he's given birth is leading him into a sinister labyrinth where he comes and goes blindfolded, his feet undermined by uncertainties. He would like to stay above the fray, manipulate the characters and structures from on high as he's learned to, but he can't, this transsexual has grabbed him with his bony hand and is forcing him down in front of him, down to the ground where the Warriors and the Bacchanalians are trading disguises and stripping him of his. When he's able to sleep, he dreams that he puts on a red dress and that his father says to him, with all the disapproval he used to be capable of, "Red looks very bad on you, Mirella."

The following day, a crushing humidity veils the sun. The slightest movement makes Thomas sweat like an Olympian. He spends the day inside, writing beneath the blades of the fan and drinking beer. When the first rolls of thunder hit the mountain at five o'clock, he has finished.

It's a colossal storm, it throws everything into anarchy and disorder, sends the world back to the first stammerings of the cosmic purée. The sky is filled with lightning, the noise is infernal, the falling water is so vertical and stiff that it becomes an offensive weapon. Standing on the balcony, Thomas watches the show. He is smiling. Then he makes her out in the opening of her door, a red stain with her back to the light. She says, "All this violence is terrifying." She comes out beside him and stands there, quaking with every burst of thunder. She says, "I'm sorry about yesterday, I'm a bit unsociable." She adds, "If the offer still holds, I'd be very happy to have a glass of Sauterne." He looks towards her. She has her arms crossed against her chest, the way women do when they're afraid and asking for protection.

He turns back to watch the storm. He doesn't answer.

MADAME BOVARY

FOR Pierre Foglia

SHE READ his newspaper column every day. She would wait until Vincent had left for the office and the school bus had picked up Caroline and Mathieu at the door, because she needed solitude and space for her reading. She would sit down at the bay window, where her eyes could angle away from the garden to the distant ghostly cross of Mont Royal. She always read his column twice, often with a smile, and sometimes with a strange pain that dug itself into her chest. Afterwards she would leave the paper open on her knees for a long time, and sip dreamily at her black coffee, which was almost cold from having waited on the carpet.

Of course he wrote well, but that wasn't what aroused her interest. What stood out was the passion in his writing—he went into rages that sent reality head over heels, and then what emerged were the shredded, indecent undergarments of an unexpected seduction. He was also insolent and cruel, he had a way of speaking that totally destroyed someone or something, just in passing. What he wrote bore no resemblance to her own universe. For example, he didn't believe in marriage and other time-tested institutions. He was always calling everything into question, even the calm foundations of existence. "A revolutionary," Vincent, who sometimes got furious reading him, would say, "a revolutionary and a Marxist," and she would agree distractedly in order not to have to defend an inexpressible opinion. Besides, she didn't know what a Marxist was.

What she knew, on the other hand, was that reading him alone, opposite the picturesque scenery and the garden ceaselessly transformed by the seasons, had a curious intoxicating effect she wouldn't have known how to do without. He was different from her, yet it was she he was addressing, her hidden self, her illicit soul. He was her secret delinquency, the nostalgia for a road she might have taken, which would have led her elsewhere, maybe far higher, well beyond that narrow cross overhanging Mont Royal.

She never dreamed she would some day meet him. Her dreams were rational and possible, which that was not. However, when she read his column that particular spring morning, she suddenly heard her pulse panic even before the words had reached her. He was writing, "Invite me to your house." He was writing, "Yes, you, Mr., Ms., or Mrs., from Saint-Télesphore or Saint-Lambert, from Percé or Nomininque, invite me. I don't drink alcohol but I like iced tea, we'll have a chat, you will be the subject of my summer columns. Columns about the ordinary world."

She lived in Saint-Lambert.

She shoved the paper into the recycling box under the week's garbage and struggled to forget what she had just read. But an hour later something peremptory forced her to retrieve the column and cut it out, the cold print was giving off something hot, something that rose like a real voice, a masculine command for her alone. *Invite me.*

She looked at herself in the mirror. Her cheeks were crimson, the way they got when she forgot to protect her delicate skin from the sun, and her violet eyes flickered anxiously. "What's wrong with you?" she asked herself, "what are you afraid of?" But the answer was obvious in her tortured reflection, floating on the surface of the mirror. She was on the verge of a terrifying parallel universe which, if she crossed into it, would never let her out.

She took her Mont Blanc, a gift from Vincent that she used only occasionally, for writing in her diary, and, opening wide the door to the terrifying parallel universe, she wrote to the Journalist.

I've been reading you for ever. I'm part of that ordinary world you would like to visit, even though I'm pretty enough that I'm sometimes taken for an actress. But beauty, as you know, is useless if it is not also interior. I think I have interior beauties to share with you. I also know how to make extraordinary Paris-Brest pastries and pies, my friends say, that it would give me great pleasure to have you sample. We could chat in my garden while looking at the irises and the pond filled with water lilies, it will give you a break from the demands of life in Montreal. My garden is at its best in June, but you can come whenever you like, before or after, I'll organize my schedule accordingly. This is the invitation I can offer you and I very much hope you will accept it.

diane

She read it over several times, twisting her lips. Putting the lower-case "d" at the start of her name almost redeemed its weakness. She suddenly remembered that the Journalist liked cats, and she traded her sentence about the pastries for "I have a cat named Paris-Brest, for the cake that my friends claim I make like no one else, you can judge for yourself." She blushed at her audacity, she who had never had a cat and didn't know how to lie, and then she hurried to seal the envelope and mail it before she changed her mind.

She didn't think about it again until night-time, beside Vincent, who had instantly collapsed into a sleep as faraway as a business trip. An important omission had come to her quite naturally in her letter, she'd spoken of herself as if she were single, she had sacrificed the existence of her children and Vincent for the sake of an imaginary cat, and for a long time she lay with her eyes open in the dark, wondering why.

After that there were days when, for no reason, she felt overjoyed, and she ate, she cooked, she listened to Vincent's soliloquies on computers, she helped Caroline with her homework and scolded Mathieu for an insolent remark, but she was elsewhere; her eyes shining and her soul airborne, she saw herself moving about from a distance, like a stranger, an old part of herself in the process of mutating. On other days, she was too afraid to eat or sleep. What had she done? How could she confront this man who was both her ideal and her silent rebellion? And she would pray that her letter had been lost or that after getting it he'd thrown it out. Time went by. Now, possessed by desire and fear, she devoured his columns without savouring them; he would talk of So-and-so in Abitibi whom he was going to meet, or another in the Upper Laurentians he was returning from, and the weeks passed with their growing light and their perfumed greens, the lilacs were scattering their blossoms on the garden and the ruby-throated hummingbirds had moved in on the irises, and she realized he would never reply to her invitation. She was saved. She was shattered.

Of course her letter was too ordinary, she herself was so ordinary she hadn't known how to project herself irresistibly. Maybe she should have included a picture with her letter, or done a better job of embellishing her situation—as the others must certainly have done, the lucky ones, those he visited and transformed by his presence. The sting of this rejection was more painful than she could have imagined. Irritable and depressed, she languished for days, despite the fact that summer had definitively arrived. Even Vincent, who never saw anything, noticed. One evening when they were alone at the table after a lobster dinner, he took her hand and talked to her about a seaside vacation. She freed her hand with a nervous laugh, she didn't want a vacation beside some stupid sea, she wanted to stay by the garden and watch all that was mortal die. While Vincent's puzzled eyes followed her she got up and ran sobbing to their bedroom. At eleven the next morning she got a call from the Journalist.

His voice was harsh, a bit mannered, more clumsy than arrogant. He didn't talk like an insolent and cynical columnist, he expressed himself very politely, with hesitations and saying "Ma'am" like an adolescent. When he had given his name she had turned to ice and fire, but gradually she became human again and succeeded in saying "How are you?" and "What an exceptional June!" with the inflections in the right place, like a person in a normal state. He suggested a meeting at her place the following week, Thursday at midday, and before agreeing she left a respectably lengthy silence, so he would think she had to deal with a busy schedule, a life full of demands from everywhere. When she hung up, her heart firm despite its palpitations, she knew she had irremediably turned into someone else.

She needed a cat.

The lie was committed, fixed in written eternity, she very urgently needed a cat, trained and willing to answer to the ridiculous name of Paris-Brest. Problem. That same night destiny winked at her: Vincent discovered a cat in the garden, so skinny its ribs showed, and was about to expel it like any other member of that unfortunate species which insisted on urinating in their greenery when she vehemently interposed herself. She wanted a cat, THIS exact cat, yes all of a sudden, absolutely, she wasn't some programmed creature, she claimed the right to nourish sudden desires and modify her preferences. Vincent, a good fellow whose love for her was greater than any of life's difficulties, was easily convinced, and the children applauded this living innovation. The cat, grey as a cliché, short-haired, one ear erased by the misfortunes of existence, apparently homeless, found itself inside the house, purring with amazement on the armchairs.

Of course she would have liked it to be prettier or less skinny, but provided he was offered food, he responded promptly to anything, even the name of a pastry. She bought kilos of kitty litter and canned meat, then noticed that Caroline, unable to breathe and her skin turning red, was terribly allergic. Paris-Brest was thus returned to the anonymity of the outdoors, weighed down with a few compensatory cans of food. Too bad, but it wasn't her first lie, now for the Journalist's benefit she would invent an accident, a sudden death. Anyway, surely he wouldn't ask to see the cat.

Now that she knew that their meeting was imminent, that she would slip through to the other side of the mirror, a great peace came over her. She had but to seize this extraordinary offer, seize the life-ring that would rescue her from the ocean of mediocrity, it was centuries since she had seized anything. She no longer felt afraid. She told Vincent, her voice firm, that she was expecting a girlfriend the following Thursday, a very dear childhood friend, this other person she had become calmly opened her mouth and the lies flowed out, fluid, airy, painless. She asked Vincent to leave her the house until evening, maybe he could drive the children to school and afterwards take them to eat at some sort of McDonald's while she and her childhood friend had their emotional reunion in the garden's oasis. Vincent approved, enthusiastic for her, she never saw anyone, and to give her more opportunity he grafted an evening at the movies onto the McDonald's. Instead of softening her, this loving credulity made her violently irritated, as though he'd shown her a weakness.

She waited for him.

All through the day she thought about him, long after reading his column; she saw, radiating from every sentence, the bond that would grow between them, she thought about him with such force that it must have reached him even down there near Mont Royal, where he was writing without knowing just how much the coming Thursday would be a revolution for him as well.

She thought about him while she travelled through her previous life, her life when she hadn't yet belonged to anyone. Despite the torrid sun she shut herself in her room and foraged through the rarely visited drawer where she kept the relics of her student days. She reconnected euphorically with her teenage self in the yearbook photographs: she was vice-president of her class, she took part in amateur theatricals, she drew well, once she'd got an A for a French composition, here was every possible proof that a magnificent future awaited her. What had broken her momentum? At what precise point had her life veered towards the disaster of banality? She found the answers in the pictures of a college party. There was Vincent, amidst the crowd, smiling like a conqueror, like someone who knew the apocalypse will follow his appearance, and she looked at this fifteen-year-old photo of Vincent with cold sadness, looked at the way the annihilator had lost in hair what he'd gained in weight.

Afterwards she tried on clothes in front of the bedroom mirror, daring dresses, expensive blouses, comfortable shorts, nothing seemed right for this decisive Thursday, nothing gave her back her old self or her broken freedom.

Wednesday she opted for a peasant skirt with a tank top. The top was so close-fitting that her breasts felt naked, and she looked at herself hard in the mirror, trying to see herself the way he would see her.

She was thirty-four years old, she was still beautiful. Her breasts had stayed high and round despite her pregnancies, and only the rebellious swell of her stomach resisted the Jane Fonda exercises she inflicted on herself every evening. When there was a barbecue around the neighbours' swimming-pool, she was the one the other men would keep sneaking looks at, the one whose body stood up best to the maximum state of undress. Her auburn hair fell freely to her shoulders, unlike all those women who hit thirty and rushed to take on the look of their old age. She had pale skin and violet eyes, a striking contrast slightly spoiled by her freckles, alas, a multiple catastrophe that had dogged her since childhood. "My little prickleberry," Vincent would call her on an evening when he was feeling sexy, but she didn't want to think about Vincent, on this eve of the revolution nothing was more misplaced than Vincent's existence.

She took off all her clothes and stood naked in front of the mirror, shivering all over beneath the cold, inquisitional stare of her violet eyes. "What do you want?" she asked herself. "What do you want from him?" Her violet eyes fluttered nervously, of course she knew what she wanted.

She wanted to sleep with him.

He arrived at exactly one in the afternoon, in a noisy rattletrap of a car. She was sitting near the door, her armpits damp with anxiety and fear. The kitchen still smelled of the chou pastry she had cooked at dawn, so that the Paris-Brest, stuffed with praline buttercream, could be as fresh as possible. Hearing the car, she stood up abruptly, then made herself sit down. Above all, she must not be subservient.

He was very tall, he almost had to bend over to shake her hand. But in spite of his intellectual's eyeglasses and his European accent, he seemed so timid and awkward that she was immediately at ease. She liked his wrinkled and badly cut clothes, she liked his sweaty odour, the Journalist who had borne her so high for so long was just an approachable human being.

Right away, he asked to see the cat.

Or rather, he asked for Paris-Brest, and she got up, somewhat confused, to get from the refrigerator the cake she'd planned to serve as a snack late in the afternoon. Neither of them laughed at the substitution, especially not her, bogged down in her bloody cat-crushed-by-schoolbus story. Bizarrely, in the face of those myopic eyes avoiding her own, it no longer seemed proper to lie. She offered him a helping of pastry, she offered him a rum and Coke, but he would only accept a glass of water, no bubbles. A sort of panic came over her at the idea that events weren't going to unfold according to plan, and she offered him a quarter-lime with such an imploring gesture that he, amazed, accepted it.

Now they were in the garden. He had started to ask her questions, since after all that was the reason for their meeting, but his questions were disconcertingly banal, and she had to labour to try to make her replies fascinating. Did the chestnut tree give edible chestnuts? What were those little blue flowers growing in the moss? Did she have to mow the lawn very often? At the end of half an hour of mental torture and overly strong rum and Coke she gave up the game, exhausted, and decided to just be herself, too bad. Miraculously, that was the moment the magic began to work.

She spoke openly, the way she used to, long ago, about the days when there were men to conquer and a universe to be tamed; once again she was the happily prattling schoolgirl, fearless and irrepressible. She told how she would sit in the light near the forget-me-nots, doing nothing for hours except floating beatifically above her body, she talked about meaningful dreams, reincarnation, astrology, and the whole time she felt his eyes on her, widened and surprised, and when she got up to renew her rum and Coke and his glass of water she saw that he looked furtively at her breasts.

Everything became easy—showing him the toad concealed under the white water lilies in the small pond, accidentally brushing his arm while telling him about her irises and finally leading him inside, into the storage-room pompously baptized a library in honour of its hundred or so books silently gathering dust. At the sight of the books he suddenly grew animated, and she watched him with a slight smile as he skipped from one book to another, amazed to see titles that were critically praised but not particularly popular. She stretched out the pleasure for a moment, then frankly admitted the library's secret: all the books in it had been praised by him at some time in his column—over the years he had made it his business to recommend certain reading and she had assiduously obeyed. She saw his eyes grow even rounder with this astonishment which was like a caress. Of course, she added with a candour whose effect she was now aware of, she'd only had time to skim through them. But one day she would read these books and eventually she would pass them on to her children as an important inheritance, because yes, she had children, even a husband sometimes.

She let Vincent's name slip with a slightly disillusioned smile, careful not to lie completely but to suggest the opening—thus, this evening the man who was accidentally her husband, this electronic doctor who took care of computer programs, would be very late getting home, but all right, she was used to these small separations that presaged, no doubt, a more definitive one.

Chewing his lip, the Journalist seemed to contemplate this information, and she wondered if she had been sufficiently explicit, and how to be more so, too much marital fidelity would definitely not pave the way for the subtleties of seduction. From the slightly shamefaced way he once more glanced at her, she saw that he was too timid and nothing would happen today. But seeds sown in fertile soil are bound to germinate; he liked women and she knew how persuasive she was, emboldened by alcohol, her breasts almost naked. Sooner or later he'd come back, but meanwhile he was running away, alarmed by the sharpness of this desire which was surely rising within him; he looked at his watch, on which the time had sped by, and thanked her for her charming hospitality. Amused, she followed him to the door. How afraid of her he was, how vulnerable despite being over six feet tall. Instead of taking his proffered hand, she kissed him near his lips, very quickly, while reminding him that he had her telephone number. His sweaty odour, pregnant and musky, was still on her a quarter-hour after he'd left, and suddenly she remembered the Paris-Brest untouched in the refrigerator. Too bad, Vincent and the children would be glad to settle for this earthly nourishment.

Poor Vincent, stretched out beside her in his comfortable pyjamas, his cuckold's pyjamas, poor Vincent who had been tenderly inquiring after this childhood friend and the reunion that she MUST follow up on, yes, he was even providing her with future alibis and he was looking at her with such unshakable confidence, his mouth still moist with praline buttercream, poor Vincent.

She would do him no harm, neither he nor the children would know anything about this adventure in which so much of her would blossom into a parallel life. Affectionate and serene, she took his hand, and she fell asleep trying to remember the Journalist's face, but all her memory could summon up was his odour, a scent of the crime.

There was no column until the following Monday. That day when she feverishly opened the paper, he was there. She had to reread it several times before she realized he was talking about her, so little, to tell the truth, barely a few lines. "I've had it," he wrote. "The columns about everyday life were a terrible idea," he wrote, "the last straw being delivered last week by a little lady from the suburbs, a pathetic humanoid appliance searching for her soul between pastry-making and astrology, a Madame Bovary far less savoury than Flaubert's. Starting tomorrow I'll be returning to my usual subject matter."

She read it, she reread it. She ran to the shopping-centre bookstore to buy this Flaubert's *Madame Bovary*, though in fact she had a copy in her ideal library. She devoured the book angrily, skipping over the infinitely long descriptions and the agricultural shows, and when she had finished she threw the book across the living-room. She didn't understand, she didn't see the connection, she saw only the contempt.

Mechanically she made herself a coffee and went to sit facing the garden, no newspaper on her knees.

Where had she gone wrong? Where was she still going wrong? Could it be that she had always been mistaken, afflicted with some imperfection so huge that she'd never been able to see it from the outside?

In front of her, the garden was exploding with colour. Sitting upright in her armchair she felt suddenly so hollow, so upset, she thought she was passing out.

So what did Emma do at the end of the book? She poisoned herself with arsenic. In books there is always a solution within reach, books lie.

In real life, whatever happens, you have to keep on living. You have to live for ever, even petrified, even empty, while imagining arsenic must have this inoffensive sickly-sweet taste, this taste of tears and black coffee.

BLACK AND WHITE

FOR Dany Laferrière

I WATCHED your movie right to the end, Malcolm X, even if it is too long and films are for women. You hurt me, brother. Your story is unreasonable. It's not until the last fifteen minutes of your life that you show a bit of judgement, when you go into Egypt and come back to Chicago and when you're being chased by black bandits, yes, I said BLACKS, brother, and suddenly you understand that the white man in general might not be the world's worst murderer and eater of pork the way you never stopped crying about from the beginning, but it's too late and you get yourself shot and I'd like to say that'll teach you. How do you expect my stupid hare-brained children to remember those fifteen minutes when the preceding three hours and twelve minutes are nothing but calls to eviscerate the white pigs?

They won't remember, that's what I'm saying. Their soft little brains have absorbed the bad parts of your life just to piss me off, and they do piss me off, you wouldn't believe how much. First of all they've painted Xs everywhere in their room, in such a black black it's imprinted there until the Last Judgement. Every day my son Gégé drives me crazy asking for big glasses like the ones you wore and I don't mean to hurt your feelings, brother, but those glasses are certainly the most horrible thing that could happen to the little face of an eleven-year-old boy who has, what's more, perfect eyesight. My daughter Julie, eight and a half years old, decided nothing would stop her from becoming a Muslim like you, until her mother explained to her that she would have to wrap herself head to foot like a caterpillar in its cocoon. Melissa is the tribe's oldest and most stubborn member, she already has her mother's bad character and I wouldn't want to be the poor Negro she sinks her claws into in a few years. Thanks to you she's discovered the word "racism" and she's wild about it. In her mind everything is racist now, including when I tell her to come home earlier on Saturday night. Her latest mania is for pasting news clippings of America's racist horrors into a scrapbook, and poisoning my one morning coffee by reading me the bloodiest extracts. A decent man who works fifteen hours straight doesn't need to start his day finding out about his brothers' every little slap in the face, you know that, brother.

But where I really disagree, what really drives me crazy, is when her mother—my wife, Flore Saint-Dieu, and you're very lucky not to know her, picks up hysterical ideas from the hysterical types you've excited with the senseless story of your life and starts seeing racism even HERE.

Here in Montreal. Get serious, my friend. If there were racism in Montreal, wouldn't I be the first to know? Since I started driving a taxi in Montreal, haven't I taken 58,456 people, three-quarters of them white, anywhere and everywhere in this city?

I'm not saying I've never met a cheater or had a hard time. But who robbed me of five hundred dollars by making me pay my driver's fee twice before taking off with his cheque as company manager? It hurts me to say this, brother, but it was a guy from Cité-Soleil like me, who called himself Magloire Charles, if you want the whole truth, and may the Devil spear his balls on a pitchfork and roast him. Who almost raped Flore Saint-Dieu—I know, it's hard to believe—when she was at the height of her former beauty, just after we got married? Bébé

Préval, an old Haitian, my friend, or, as you say, a Caribbo-Quebecker. Who, for twenty lousy dollars, just murdered our friend Nizafed at the wheel of his taxi? A young creep by the name of Barry Bishop, as black as your first mistress was white, take that!

The facts speak for themselves, men prey on other men, whether they're black, yellow or Martian green. That doesn't suit Flore Saint-Dieu, she changes reality the way she does just for the pleasure of contradicting me. You know how women are, brother, and at what distance they become charming again, you found out soon enough to stay far away from your own even though she was pretty cute.

Once, when he was leaving school, our son Gégé was called "a little black shit" and got his nose broken by a skinhead. So what does a sensible creature do to console her child? Does she rush off screaming like a madwoman to SOS Racism, which is of course what our son's mother did? If you want my advice, friend, a sensible creature wipes the bleeding nose and says, "Son, whether you like it or not, life is full of violence, it's time you learned to defend yourself." Another time Melissa added to the scrapbook of her morning jeremiads that in her college cafeteria the whites never sit at the same tables as the Haitians—but notice, brother, the opposite is equally true, another way of putting it is that the Haitians at her college never sit at the same table, etc., but try explaining that to a fired-up adolescent who's just been to see *Malcolm X* for the third time, forgetting the decisive last fifteen minutes every time. Okay. Does a sensible father file a complaint with the Ministry of Education? The answer is self-evident: a father who is sensible and has a sense of humour keeps on drinking his one coffee and sighs that he too would give anything, some mornings, not to sit beside his dear dog-brained daughter. Another time, in the bus she takes to Outremont to clean house for the rich, Flore got called a "monkey" by a white woman. How does a sensible husband react when his wife reports this incident? He sure doesn't laugh in front of her, I can tell you that now, my friend, because that's what I did and my left cheek still burns where she slapped me.

What I'm saying is that you can't lump everything together. Sure, lots of little things have happened to me that it would be easy to stupidly attribute to racism instead of to surprise. But brother, surprise is a great destabilizer of human beings. Take any human being, my friend, take you: there you are with your two arms and two legs and you're waiting for someone you don't know for a meeting or one of your Muslim things, and a legless cripple shows up in front of you; you're surprised, perhaps you go so far as to look down on him and even risk a little joke, nothing could be more normal. Replace the legless cripple with someone of another colour and you understand everything. Of course, some people never get over the unexpected; others immediately see that you're a decent hard-working man just like them despite the missing limbs or orange or frizzy hair. Decent men can always recognize each other.

I'm telling you, brother, you should have come to live in Montreal. Here it would have been easy for you to go to your quiet little mosque, and you might even have become a television personality. Look at our brother Dany, who's a king in Montreal. Our brother Dany is the same age as me, and the same as you just before you got yourself shot. He wrote that book *How to Get Tired in the Dark with a Negro* which I'm going to read one of these days, and red carpets and beautiful women spread themselves out in front of him. Do you think that would have been possible in a city swept by the white breath of racism, as Flore Saint-Dieu stupidly says? Our brother Dany doesn't bow and scrape and that's why he's a king.

Every time I see him on television my heart swells with pride, and I can feel the warm breeze of Port-au-Prince. The others, despite their television make-up, look like anemic junior officers beside him, because wherever he goes the sun goes with him, the sun and laughter. *Mwen renmen l'.* I love him.

Laughter, that's what you've been missing, my poor friend Malcolm. If a bit of humour had lightened up your view through those big glasses, God knows where you'd be today. Maybe in Montreal, your two feet in the snow instead of underground.

It's true, brother, that colour becomes important in the snow. When the snow is brown, life is disgusting. But when the snow is white, Montreal seems like a young bride. When the snow is truly white, that's when it's easy, that's when I can walk in it pretending that it's sand, that Flore Saint-Dieu's hand is soft in mine again, that it's sand leading to the warm and fragrant sea.

SOMETHING DIFFERENT

———————————

AHEAD IT'S blue. With layers of light that shimmer until your eyes are blinded. Above Jeanne it's also blue, except when the waving palm trees nibble furtively at the sky. Something warm and fragrant emanates from the sea and is carried everywhere. Jeanne, held by her hammock as by a gentle lover, sways in the warmth and fragrance.

Here, thoughts are weightless, memory is a feather that passes over every reef. In so distant Montreal, its name as scratchy as steel wool, in another life, Jeanne had a cat, a profession, a man named Claude. At least that's what she thinks, she remembers, vaguely. Here the air is too light to possess anything; when Claude's face attempts to break the surface, it has no more mouth, no expression, it floats in an unreal fog, totally inoffensive.

Far away on the beach, slender silhouettes move about, tourists she knows are mostly Quebeckers. Jeanne stays here where they don't come. Last week one of them got his skull cracked open by a coconut; since then they stay away from the palms, terrified by this vegetal bombardment never mentioned in the travel brochures.

But here are two of them, and they seem to be advancing towards her. For a moment Jeanne spies on these audacious intruders through her sunglasses. A man and a woman, very tanned, their shapes pleasant to the eye. They are walking quickly, they'll eventually pass her and dissolve into the horizon. When Jeanne opens her eyes later, the man and woman are standing motionless in front of her, facing the sea.

The man has blond hair and a bandanna knotted Indian-style around his forehead. On his shoulder he is carrying a large wicker basket covered in multicoloured cloth. The woman has luxuriant black hair and isn't carrying anything; except for her bathing suit which is reduced to the bare minimum. They are very handsome together, an Inca Scandinavian twinning that shines in the sun. They talk to each other softly without looking, in an incomprehensible singsong language. Jeanne perks up her ears. Maybe it's their voices, or the way they have of abruptly piling on the words: a drama is in the making.

Suddenly the woman lets out a sob; she runs from the shore, brushes against Jeanne and stops for a few seconds. Her eyes are black and despairing. Jeanne, disturbed, gets up from her hammock, but the woman has already disappeared behind the palms and almond trees. The man follows her slowly, the basket swaying on his shoulder. He doesn't stop in front of Jeanne, but as he passes he gives her an apologetic smile and a green feline look.

Later, while swimming in the sea, Jeanne catches sight of them sitting tranquilly beneath the almond trees. They are looking out towards her, or towards the sea, it's impossible to tell. Jeanne wanders for a moment along the shore, where the surf has uncovered living sand dollars that glow like pebbles. She suddenly hears a yelping that fixes her to the spot, a wild cry that deafens the almonds. She sees them leaning solicitously over the wicker basket. The noise stops.

Even later, rocked by the hammock, Jeanne lets herself slide into a brief doze, and when she opens her eyes the man, the woman and the wicker basket have disappeared. The mugginess empties out of the day.

Now Jeanne is drinking a piña colada while she watches the

spectacle of the red sun drowning in the sea. Other Quebeckers are sitting on the terrace, but to avoid the hateful overtures of compatriots Jeanne pretends she speaks only Spanish. From the forest come sweet and haunting odours. It's the time of day when saki monkeys and sloths start moving around in the mangroves. A pair of toucans nonchalantly survey the bay with quick proprietary glances.

Jeanne notices a woman who is dancing, farther out on the beach. She is inhabited by some kind of magic that makes her turn in the light. Jeanne recognizes her right away. Her eyes search for the other, with his pale hair. At this exact moment a waiter presents Jeanne with another piña colada, encircled by a hibiscus flower. Surprised, she turns her head; the blond man is on the terrace, a few metres away from her. He sends her an oblique smile filled with disturbing implications. The sun dives abruptly and almost immediately everything goes dark, everything falls rustling into the tropical night.

Jeanne lights the outside lamp of her *cabina*: a colony of insects gathers instantaneously, as though obeying a rallying cry. Jeanne knows the man and the woman occupy the neighbouring *cabina*. A little while ago she saw them moving in, she saw how insistently they kept looking in her direction. She waits. The voracity of this expectation frightens her. Something is going to happen, something she's afraid to hurry.

What happens is a cry, the same ear-splitting squealing as at the beach. Jeanne hurries outside. She doesn't make him out right away, he's staying in the dark, but he's betrayed by his white shirt.

"Don't be afraid," he says, "it's the kipichu."

"The what?"

He expresses himself in a musical French, coloured with an

indefinable accent. He explains that the kipichu is their pet, a jungle creature they found and tamed.

"It's a small nocturnal mammal like a cat and a monkey at the same time. It's very affectionate, and very noisy."

"That's what you take walking in the basket?"

"Yes."

He laughs. He says the kipichu is a tyrant who doesn't accept being left alone. He also says that kipichus are on their way to extinction. "Like our people," he adds briefly, and stops laughing.

A soft light comes on in the veranda, simultaneously revealing the theatrical silhouette of the woman, draped in a flamboyant brocade that turns her almost phosphorescent. She looks at Jeanne with a sphinx-like smile.

"Ther," the man says, introducing her with a courteous gesture, "Ther and Jampi."

They wait, formal and silent, for her to deign to introduce herself in turn. Impressed, Jeanne doesn't react immediately. Then she says her name in a sort of embarrassed stammer, mortified by its banality.

"Jhhann," the woman repeats, gently bowing her head in appreciation.

They start talking in that unknown language with its undulating vowels, meanwhile keeping their eyes on her. No doubt it's some sort of native dialect, and bizarrely Jeanne does not feel excluded.

"Ther says she really likes your inner light," the man translates, smiling.

Now Jeanne is sitting between the two of them, wrapped in the gilded luminescence of the veranda and the emanations from their bodies. She is happy, spellbound, these strangers overflow with a humanity she's never known before. In front of them on the table a sliced pineapple imperiously scents the air, starfruit are soaking in dark rum, and Jeanne is eating greedily, as if each mouthful contains a portion of paradise lost. Ther and Jampi talk and laugh in their language and they keep brushing her arm innocently as they speak. The kipichu's basket is suspended from the ceiling. Inquisitive, Jeanne wants to go over to it, but Jampi's hand restrains her.

"He isn't there," he says. "He's running in the jungle. But I'll show him to you. Tomorrow."

His hand stays put; it's incredibly tanned and soft. Jeanne knots up with anxiety. All this is dangerous—the hand and the rum, Ther's complicitous smile, the overwhelming perfume of the pineapple and the man's voice, dangerous, suddenly familiar, announcing that there will be a tomorrow. Dangerously irresistible.

The woman suddenly gets up, a moan in her throat, and starts to run towards the forest, crying out. Worried, Jeanne watches as Ther disappears into the darkness, then rises as though to follow. Jampi's hand pulls her back down.

"Leave her," he says. "It's nothing. The jungle is calling her, she's always in communion with the jungle. When the trees complain, she suffers. In my country we know we belong to the earth, we live connected to our roots."

At any other time such words would make Jeanne burst out laughing, but Jampi's smile is serious and his hand winds into Jeanne's neck with an animal grace. These people are crazy, of course, logically speaking they must be crazy, but now this man's body is so close to hers, now craziness takes on a new face and becomes her own life, the little grey life she and Claude plod through on Montreal's concrete. "Come with us," he breathes, while from afar she hears the kipichu's squealing and Ther's understanding laugh. "Come live with us," he commands, and she says yes, she says yes to everything, to total revolution, to something different, the sugary odour of this man's body which is slowly covering her own.

The next day Jeanne wakes up in her *cabina*. She takes the time to make sure that the sun and the tropical forest are real, to remember that the night indeed existed. She has a headache. She smells of rum and pineapple juice.

The *cabina* next door is empty, of course. They left at dawn, taking everything with them, the charlatans: their suitcases and the magic they dispensed by the shovelful. Everything?...No. They left a pineapple on the table, the kipichu's basket in a corner and a torn luggage ticket on the ground.

The basket contains these few words: "Thanks for playing with us," and a little stuffed monkey, ugly and puny like the ones sold to tourists. The suitcase ticket bears the following identification, worn away by use: THÉRèse and JEAN-PIerre Cotnoir, 7881 rue Saint-Denis, Montréal.

On the other hand, close inspection reveals the pineapple to be deliciously authentic, and Jeanne devours it on the spot while laughing to herself.

THE LABOURING CLASS

YOU WEREN'T expecting to find her there. Neither was she, obviously; she cuts short the love song she was in the midst of carolling, she almost drops her feather duster, she watches you come in with her mouth open in such terror that you'd turn and leave if you weren't in your own house.

You left work very early this afternoon; it was a stirring, lyrically sunny day and you wandered here and there, buying a few things, and now you're back; besides, you do NOT have to explain yourself to your cleaning lady, who has finally gotten hold of herself again. She helps you haul your innumerable parcels into the kitchen. She cautiously feels your bag from La Mer.

"Oh look, it's moving," she cries.

"Lobsters, Madame Saint-Dieu."

You know that her name is Flore Saint-Dieu and that she's Haitian. That's all you know about her, that and the fact that she comes once a week to clean your house. You take from her hands the scented Dans un Jardin cream that she was about to put in the refrigerator—"The bag is so pretty, I thought it must be a cake," she apologizes—and you persuade her, as well as can be expected, to get back to her usual tasks. And while you find places in your already jammed refrigerator to store your kilo of smoked salmon, your Chez Le Nôtre pastries, your two Boursault cheeses, your dozen figs at two fifty each, you catch her eyes lingering—oh, just for a fraction of a second—on the receipts you negligently dropped on the corner of the table.

You go into your office. She's already there, wiping each of the slats of your vertical anthracite-grey blind. It promises to take a long time. You aren't too sure how to act with her, her presence irritates you, like some kind of boil in its terminal stage. But she makes it easier, she becomes like the blind, silent and grey. You forget her. You pick up the telephone. You argue for a while with your travel agent about your next trip to the Seychelles. Then you give your accountant a hard time about some investments that have stopped going up. You trade erudite jokes with the principal of the private school your son attends. When you finally put down the receiver, Madame Saint-Dieu is still there beside you, she is carefully dusting the globe and it seems to you she's putting extra time into the blue zones.

You sit down in your favourite armchair, near the doorway. You look at everything harmonious in this comfortable corner of your house: the nineteenth-century table with its pale golden wood that trembles in the light, the standing lamp with its carved pedestal, that large Yves Bussières drawing with its daring line, even the garments hanging from the coat-peg—your wife's dark beaver coat, your Chapuis Dubuc jacket—but...THAT? Suddenly you notice something unspeakable, yellowish and hairy, a horribly garish coat with a fake fur collar hung, as if nothing could be more normal, right in the midst of your beautiful things. You feel sick, you get up to unhook the thing.

"That's my coat!"

You didn't hear her coming but there she is in front of you, overflowing with Cyclopean rage.

"Not so pretty, is it? Poor people's coats are never pretty."

You suddenly understand that you won't be able to get out of this, you've been going to the sea for too long and she hasn't been back for too long, you've been feasting on lobster while she's had to subsist on rice, her children have been shivering in cheap sweaters while yours reject their worn Lacostes. Madame Saint-Dieu is standing in front of you, made tall by all the filth you've had her clean up. In the corners of her eyes she wears the star emblem of the revolution, she brandishes your best knife, a scrupulously sharpened Zwilling & Henckels, and sinks it into your heart...

You wake up sweating in your favourite armchair, near the doorway. Madame Saint-Dieu is vacuuming in a distant room. When she comes to leave, wrapped up in her yellowish coat, you offer her a raise.

"How much?" she asks.

She doesn't seem surprised; a shadow of a smile slides across her lips and makes its way up to her eyes, where she has a small wrinkle you've never noticed, shaped like a star.

AURORA MONTREALIS

THEY ARE fat. They are stupid. In the evenings they fill the streets and knock a ball about, with their hockey sticks hitting everything including the parked cars. Sundays they set off in hordes for church, starched and submissive and a head taller than their mothers in black, solemn cucumbers determined to marinate in the vinegar of childhood. The one who seems to be the gang leader is the fattest and stupidest of all, which is how things are in the Kingdom of Babel. The gang leader gives Laurel a dark contemptuous look whenever the sidewalk brings them together. In Laurel's book, to get back at him, he'll always be called Soufflaki.

Laurel writes down everything. He just moved to the district a week ago, but already ten pages of his notebook are overflowing with notes and crossings-out. In three months he will have amassed enough material to start a book, a real book about the real and desolate face of the new Montreal. Being sixteen years old doesn't mean you can't have vision. "Son," his father sometimes says to him, between two puffs of grass and three strokes of the paintbrush, "you are older and better than me, you are fifty-six years old because you've already understood what it's like to be my age as well as yours."

His father has been painting, teaching, smoking grass, laughing and sleeping on the plateau Mont-Royal since Laurel's prehistory. His father comes from an old Francophone family, is one of those stubborn termites that the Anglophone and allophone tides have been unable to evict from the primordial tunnel. (And whose existence it's now inappropriate to mention, thinks Laurel.)

His mother is a different kettle of fish.

His mother could be anything at all, given the way she comes to terms with all things foreign, plunges her malleable roots into all sorts of dubious compost. His mother lives in the Greek district on the border of the Hassid district, has a natural-foods store in the English district, does her shopping from Italians and sleeps with a Chilean. In Laurel's book she'll be called Universalle and she'll die early on, a victim of assassination or assimilation.

Laurel closes his notebook, but doesn't yet risk going outside. Outside, Soufflaki and some of his flabby acolytes occupy the territory, wearing their inline skates. The confrontation will come soon enough, better to examine the adversary first and secretly prepare his weapons. Soufflaki is wearing a long T-shirt over his quivering belly, and on the back is an inscription which is swirling too quickly to be legible. He skates well, the animal. When his mother appears in the door across the street and shouts something in their patois, the back of his T-shirt becomes sufficiently still that Laurel can read: *I'm not deaf, I'm ignoring you.*

The mothers of Soufflaki and his kind have strident voices that they throw into the street like grenades. The fathers are more discreet. Soufflaki's stands in the window in the middle of the day, contemplatively picking his nose.

Still wearing his skates, Soufflaki disappears into his house. It's the signal for the others to disperse, and finally the way is clear.

Laurel goes out. Since the beginning of this week spent in Universalle's dense recesses, he has learned to walk without stopping and without distraction, a feverish guerrilla tracking incriminating signs. Avenue du Parc, for example, is a linguistic battleground, a micro-Babel booming out ugliness. Invariably Laurel slows in front of the computer stores where all sorts of *hardwares compatibeules* are to be found, the rug merchants with their *beautiful tapis*, and their *merveilleux carpettes de Turkish*. They are degenerate. They are *incredibeul*. Staring through the window, scornful and angry, he takes out his notebook and slashes it with vengeful phrases—often while being looked at by the owner, who gives him a hesitant smile, unclear about his intentions but taking no chances. Once, ambushed in front of a snack bar, *Nous fésons les potines tostés*, Laurel noticed a boy his own age also holding a pad and frantically taking notes. Overcoming his usual reserve, Laurel quickly moved to stand beside him, his hand almost extended and his heart softening with the beginning of an authentic friendship—battle companion, oh my brother, will we be on the same side of the barricade?...Suspicious, the boy took off his Walkman headphones—*Whadayawant?*—and Laurel saw what he was so intent on copying down, it was the words of a song whose *very hard metal* and *terribly English* vibrations now spread freely into the street. Oops. *Exquiouse me*.

All right, he is alone, he has suspected it for a long time and maybe one day he'll end up getting used to it. He is alone, an exception to the idiotic statistics and stereotypes, he is not the garish, illiterate teenager without a cause that the sociologists have established as the norm and the newspapers are always denouncing. They are morons. Why, at sixteen any more than at fifty, would everyone be the same?

He has no inline skates and he refuses to like mountain bikes. He has never slept with a girl. He reads instead of watching television, he reads Quebec French books to the exclusion of all others. He knows Michel Tremblay by heart, he has taken his image of Montreal as Babel from Francine Noël, he venerates Sylvain Trudel and Gaétan Soucy and

Esther Rochon and Louis Hamelin. And he has found his Cause, to which he will devote all his new and recycled energy: to defend French Montreal against the Invaders.

It's not easy, it's not smooth going, especially with the soothing Universalle who doesn't see any enemies and would sell her soul to communicate. Since they've started living together again, there's no way to have a real conversation with her, a confrontation worth the bother. He points out the irrefutable problems and innumerable perils threatening their city; smiling, she listens to Laurel, as if he weren't a worthy adversary, she never raises her voice, she strokes his cheek making him want to bite. "You're a clever little bugger, but you'll change," she says, smiling.

He would kill her if he didn't love her so much, poor blind sheep running to her own death, he'll content himself with killing her in his book so she'll finally understand the real dangers he wanted to spare her.

Real dangers have infiltrated everywhere and taken every form. Sometimes they have nothing to do with language and, even worse, wear spiritual clothing. All these displays of religion—veils, turbans, kepis, rolls, crosses and salaams that flourish around Laurel are for him a subtle menace, an obstacle to the most fundamental freedom, the freedom to believe in nothing and to feel, why not, like shit.

On avenue du Parc there's a Syrian pastry shop with rosewater and pistachio cream baklavas that make an unforgettable impression. Since the beginning of the week Laurel has been there twice, and he is going back today. This Syrian is a short affable man who speaks impeccable French and welcomes customers as if they were long-lost friends. Too bad. Every time he is about to mention money, he bows low, his hands shaped like a tent in front of his forehead, and offers some barbarous Moloch or Tanith a silent prayer ("Lord, how much should I ask for these delicious sesame biscuits?" or "Lord, take this two dollars and ninety-five cents and add it to the three hundred and ten thousand dollars and forty cents already given for the salvation of my soul.") It's irritating. Every time he finds himself witnessing this untimely devotion, Laurel muzzles his annoyance by thinking about the creamy promises of the baklava. Today—he doesn't know where he gets the nerve—just as the little Syrian, immobile in front of his cash register, puts his hands to his forehead, Laurel sarcastically interrupts: "Could I know just what you're saying to Him?" The little Syrian straightens up, friendly and curious, his hands still making a tent, and suddenly Laurel understands. It's not a question of fanaticism but of commerce, the pastry-maker is simply shielding the figures on his screen from the light so he can read them, it's as simple and prosaic as that. Angry at himself, Laurel leaves quickly after stammering his goodbye, and the rosewater baklava that he stuffs down without chewing seems for the first time infinitely too sweet.

Luckily, there is Mont Royal. Even before, when Laurel lived on rue Rachel with his father, he would often disappear into the wooded slopes of this small mountain—more hill than mountain, to tell the truth—turning lazily on itself instead of being in any hurry to show its summit. Mont Royal has become even more accessible from Universalle's apartment, a consolation of greenery and harmony after five hundred metres of visual disappointments. Now, as during his childhood, when Laurel is on Mont Royal his solitude becomes a sparkling cloak. He is a prince, sad like all those tied to a demanding fate, methodically pacing his kingdom while around him idiotic joggers and insane cyclists rush towards their heart attacks. He is an adventurer of slowness; no sudden rustling, no movement of the trees or wind escapes him. All kinds of surprises are in store for someone who takes the lesser paths of Mont Royal, slowly, attentively. Once Laurel saw an albino squirrel stretched out on the trunk of a maple tree like an old crust of snow. Once he found a perfect, empty wasp nest on the ground, a miracle of delicate architecture that he still possesses. Once he lay down in some poison ivy, and for two years his legs burned with the memory. Once he surprised seven raccoons talking around a full garbage can. Once, in the midst of the wild lily of the valley, he harvested a twenty-dollar bill wrapped around a cube of hashish. Once he stumbled on two naked men masturbating each other. On Mont Royal, you can never predict just what kind of amazing things you will find.

But for Laurel, during these winding ascents that finally take him to the still place where the mountain meets the city, the most amazing thing is gradually feeling a stranger move into his mind—and discovering that he likes this stranger. It's hard to be a melancholy prince and an enraged prince at the same time. Sitting at the top of Mont Royal, Laurel floats in a fog, a sweet sad prince devoid of all anger. He watches some old Portuguese men with rotten teeth having a snack in the distance, and he finds them handsome. He looks at how the city challenges the river with its skyscrapers and he finds it has the graceful modernity of a postcard. From here, Montreal is harmless.

Today the sky is vast and clear, the birches wave their scented leaves, life lies ahead at a frightening remove. Laurel chews a stalk of grass. So when will he be happy? When will he fall into the arms of a fascinating woman or an exciting career, when will he start really living, when? From above he figures out which street is his, a jagged ribbon along the sides of the park, and he sees the building where Soufflaki lives, grey but shining in the sun. Soufflaki's name raises something unpleasant within him, a dagger of irritation. The noble prince spits out his grass and his lethargy. Soufflaki! Soufflaki! Soufflaki! "One day," Laurel says to himself, "he's going to punch me in the face."

He takes his red notebook out of his bag and opens it at random. The light moves on the virgin paper and, if he looks at it a long time without blinking, fires coloured shadows that look like aurora borealis. Suddenly the title of his book appears to him, flashing on the white page. *Aurora Montrealis.* His book will be called *Aurora Montrealis*, because, he hears himself explaining, a cigarette in his mouth—he doesn't smoke but he'll have to one day, if he wants to project a strong, nonchalant image—because Montreal is a city that never stops changing—the journalists frantically scribble everything while he takes a few manly drags—a city that adds so many new faces that we always lose the one we finally thought we knew—an especially pretty journalist gives him an ecstatic smile and another sneaks him her telephone number. They are crazy about him.

Once he's at the top of the mountain, he has only to walk another half-hour to come out at the slope opposite Beaver Lake and finally onto avenue Decelles, where Universalle has her health-food store.

The store's customers are almost all Anglophones, and it's called Nature, which is pronounced *Nétchioure*, mouth rounded like a doughnut hole. This summer Universalle is thinking of opening a café adjoining the store, in which Laurel could commence his remunerated public life.

Pushing open the door, Laurel senses that he has arrived at a bad time. Universalle and her Chilean are alone in the store, but they are taking up all available atoms of space. Their faces are very close to each other, as though about to kiss or bite. Only the Chilean turns his eyes towards Laurel and smiles at him. "Hola!" he says. Hola yourself. Universalle keeps her head bent, her discreet way of showing that she's crying.

Of course he's always been bad for her, this too-handsome Hola who doesn't know how to say "Hello" even after years in Quebec, of course he was born to make her cry. A man with eyes like that can't be faithful, eyes like soft black lakes when they touch down on his mother and imprison her, cesspool eyes whose trap no woman can ever have escaped.

"Pedro is going back to Santiago," Universalle says, bravely raising her haggard face to Laurel. Hola takes her in his arms, Hola croons her name with liquid intonations, "Pôline," he says, "you will come and be with me, Pôline," and that can't be serious, said that way, with so many sugary rollings of vowels. Besides, even Universalle-Pauline shrugs her shoulders to show she isn't fooled by the absurdity of this proposal, this crooning love song.

Hola lights a cigarette. He must be happy that Laurel is there to share the drama and dilute it, his swampy eyes keep trying to catch Laurel's. Laurel watches him obliquely, just enough to see how he smokes. Hola has his own style of smoking, very aristocratic, he uses all his fingers to hold his cigarette and, when he expels the smoke, he raises his head slightly towards some invisible people and blows hard, an aristocratic or macho style, hard to know which, but when Laurel smokes, one day, that's how he wants to do it. Universalle, who doesn't smoke, also lights herself a cigarette, and smokes it nervously, any way at all, while making her forehead wrinkle to keep from crying.

Laurel knows he should leave now, he's come in on the middle of something that doesn't concern him and isn't over yet, and his being here is keeping the abscess from completely bursting open. But he stays, on purpose, staring fixedly at Universalle. I told you so, they come here, they take everything and they leave. Those are the words he doesn't have the right to say, he throws their unformulated seed at her with all his strength. She catches it. Her face becomes very pale, she stops smoking, she speaks to Laurel in an icy voice: "Go away, Laurel. Here, go eat some sushi, I'll give you the money, go."

He doesn't accept the money she holds out to him as though he were a beggar, he goes without turning back and he slams the door, his mother is chasing him away, she has always liked foreigners better than him, always.

Fortunately, yes, there is sushi. Along with Mont Royal, sushi is still the best thing about Montreal, sushi and Mont Royal are the two oases that make this inhospitable Babel almost bearable. Before, when he lived with his father on rue Rachel, on Sundays they often used to go to the Mikado on rue Laurier and everything was terrific and unforgettable, playing with the baguettes, sampling the powerful horseradish and the small candy-coloured fish. Sometimes his mother would join them for the occasion, drink too much sake, take his father's arm as though constant fighting hadn't driven them apart, as though their family puzzle still had all its pieces.

Now Laurel doesn't need to be with someone to eat sushi and know what he likes. He likes the yellow-tailed tuna, the sweet sea urchins and the psychedelic sunrise that explodes in the mouth, he likes the California rolls, he likes the taste of freshwater eel marrow and the luxuriant fire of the kamikazes, he likes to finish with a cone of spicy tuna, and he needs all that, always, in the same order, all these indispensable feast items, which cost him all his savings.

And he likes watching the Japanese, most of all he likes sitting at the counter confronting the enigma of their faces.

These Japanese laugh a lot, as though working were a big joke, they laugh while manipulating the sticky rice, the algae leaves and the pastel fish which turn to jewels in their fingers, and while they work and joke they follow everything with their vigilant, mirthful eyes, they never fail to greet important customers by name, their voices loud, their bows respectful. That's what Laurel watches for on their faces, this abrupt transition from impishness to vigilance, this covering up of one mask by another without ever revealing their true features. Maybe he is an enigma for them too. But perhaps, on the other hand, they saw through him right away, him and all the other doltish customers eternally demanding the same dishes, maybe they are very strong, endowed with a remarkable ability to adapt that makes them put on the right face at the right time.

"They are here the way they will be everywhere," Laurel writes in his red notebook. And he would go further, find other harsher words to condemn their impenetrability, but the waiter has arrived and is setting the jewelled delicacies before him with a smile, so he closes his notebook and forgets everything, on his tongue the flying-fish eggs explode against the quail's-egg yolk and the salty taste of the scallop, he closes his eyes and he forgets the melancholy city; his mouth full of tasty contrasts, he forgets Universalle's face, so sad, so hostile; in a state of extreme sensual pleasure he forgets that life is ugly and that he has enemies.

True enemies don't let themselves be forgotten for long.

When he is walking home in the half-light, Laurel gradually makes out black silhouettes gliding along the sidewalk, ghosts on wheels. He slows down, but it's too late to go back. The silhouettes come towards him, swaying and threatening. They are armed. They are fat. They are five. Like an idiot he has walked right into the centre of their web.

Laurel clutches his notebook, a pathetic shield. He watches as they describe their concentric circles around him, closer and closer. Soufflaki detaches himself from the group and casually performs a few mid-air turns before braking in front of him.

The street is the image of life: black and indifferent. He has never been so alone, but maybe one day he'll end up getting used to it.

Soufflaki comes closer. He says a few words, perhaps in Greek, since Laurel doesn't understand. Fists clenched, ready to leap, Laurel makes him repeat himself. *"What?"*

"Welcome to Montreal," Soufflaki says. Laurel looks at them one at a time; he feels the way he does at a play, or eating sushi in front of the enigmatic Japanese. Weirdly, the five boys have smiles across their faces.

Later, night floods into Laurel's room, but he is still not asleep. He can hear his mother sobbing indistinctly, like the cooing of an exotic bird. Laurel doesn't understand what he's feeling, this hole in the centre of himself, this abyss of uncertainty and ignorance. He has thrown his red notebook into the garbage. He knows nothing, he must start again from scratch. The only thing he knows is that he has to get up now, and go take Pauline in his arms to console her.

OUI OR NO

THIS IS the story of a woman who meets a man without really meeting him. There are many stories about women who meet men without really meeting them, too many, I know. But here's one more, one for the road.

This is also the story of a small confused country embedded in a large flabby one. The small country has no official papers to prove that it really is a country. It has everything else that makes a country, but the papers—those it doesn't have. Sometimes it relaxes peacefully in the bed of the large flabby country and dreams that it's at home. Sometimes it dreams that the large flabby country clutches it and swallows it up in its swampy sheets and it wakes up before disappearing.

The woman in this story lives in the small country. Her name is Éliane. For years she has been living with Philippe, whom she likes to call Filippo, for reasons she's forgotten. When the story begins, she is stretched out on the sofa while Filippo plays with the television remote control. She is watching Filippo but she is thinking about Nick Rosenfeld, with whom she slept last week. It's the moment when the day subsides into itself, ethereal and exhausted. It's also the moment when the small country speaks, on the television.

It's about what could be a historic moment. The small country has woken up and discovered that it's suffocating; to escape the stifling embraces, it's demanding a bed of its own. That requires the proper papers, charts, maps, a diploma certifying that it is indeed a country. But. It turns out that the papers don't come free, in fact they are very expensive, sacrifices will be necessary. Therefore the small country consults its people, consult, consult. It asks, "Will you allow us to buy the papers which will allow us to be sufficiently legal to allow us to have a bed of our own? Yes or no." When everyone has been consulted there will be a final consultation; then finally everyone will go to sleep.

Last week they were also talking about the small country, just before Nick Rosenfeld's mouth took hold of her fingers and began to devour them in a way that was as audacious as it was surprising. After that they didn't talk about anything. From the other side of the window shone the illuminated letters on top of the Toronto Star building. She would not have imagined that Nick Rosenfeld's mouth, so cold and intelligent, could turn into a sexual organ. She would not have imagined feverish words in this mouth possessed by discourse. *(Oh Éliane. My dear. Oh you. You.)* What one doesn't imagine but happens anyway is a powerful drug.

Every evening, on television, the small country sums up the state of the consultations. All the details can also be followed in the newspapers, but television is better for showing real passion lighting up real faces. And then, television has Philippe-Filippo. Prerecorded, he gives the commentaries and puts the questions. The Filippo beside Éliane on the sofa isn't exactly the television Philippe. The one on television stays smiling and imperturbable no matter what unfolds around him. The one beside Éliane gets carried away and fulminates and sometimes his uncontrollable emotion drowns out his own television voice.

Emotion is a volatile substance that ignites quickly in the inhabitants of this small country. Perhaps it's the fault of their Latin ancestors. For example, a little while ago on the telephone, well before Filippo came home, emotion left Éliane breathless. *(Hello, Éliane. It's Nick Rosenfeld. Is this a good time to call?...)* And during the thirty minutes of the call it got worse, neither her breath nor her ability to form sentences returned. Nick Rosenfeld's voice made an inescapable road into her ear, as warm and assured as a pillar, as a sexual organ. *(When are you coming back to Toronto?)*

The television Philippe is calmly listening to some fellow citizens of the little country who are hemming and hawing, weighing, worrying. Is it really necessary to change? Won't a new bed be too hard, too small, too big? Isn't it scary to sleep alone? How can we be sure we won't have nightmares? Aren't there less draconian ways to escape being kicked and asphyxiated? Why not just hang onto the edge of the old mattress? Why not stuff ourselves with sleeping pills? The Filippo beside Éliane in the living-room explodes with the anger so masterfully absent from his television performance. "Listen to them," he says to Éliane. "Listen to the sound of their dignity and their greatness. Brave sheep," he grinds out. "That's what they deserve to be known as, brave sheep." Éliane shares Filippo's convictions. Éliane is like Filippo. At what exact moment does a couple move away from being passionate towards being alike?

Nick Rosenfeld and Éliane are light-years apart. Now where is the space they shared so heatedly? When she hears his voice again on the telephone, several days later, this space appears in front of her as the only habitable territory. She no longer sees her computer screen, the familiar walls that shelter her universe, she no longer knows where she is, once again she's a conquered and transported body that Nick Rosenfeld keeps probing with his tongue and his sex, voraciously searching for something he never tires of not finding. He pronounces her name "Alien," like the space monster, like the foreigner each of them is to the other. She doesn't understand everything he says. What she does understand is what he wants so badly. He wants to go back with her, as soon as possible, to that fiery country without border or nationality, where, finally rid of compromise and inessentials, it's so good to burn. *(Are we going to let THIS die? When are you coming back to Toronto?)*

The small country, in spite of itself, has created its first victim. During a consultation hearing, a man fervently proclaimed that for the first time he was participating in something important; then he collapsed, felled by a heart attack. Lying fraternally side by side, Filippo and Éliane talk about this. Victims never choose the place they are going to be taken. For the first time, Éliane feels bothered by Filippo's body warmth. For the first time she feels he is in danger. She presses her body against him to protect him from Nick Rosenfeld. Danger. *Jeopardy*. For a long time, until she looked it up in the dictionary, she thought *jeopardy* was a kind of leopard.

They always talk in his language, though he says he understands hers. Of course conversation is fraught with peril, because she must pick her way around the traps of both emotion and foreign words. Every time Nick Rosenfeld puts down the receiver at his end, she searches in the dictionary and finds, too late, what she should have said to him, and she prepares terribly effective sentences that evaporate as soon as she goes to pronounce them. *(Your accent is adorable.)* The conversation is perilous and unequal. When after laborious twists and turns she finally manages to explain the distress his voice over the telephone causes her, and the terrible fear resulting from this distress, his reply is stunning. *(Same here.)* Oh, his tongue is so succinct, like punches. How to resist a tongue that goes straight to what it wants and lingers so long in memory? *(Oh Éliane. My dear. Oh you. You.)*

Expectations are a source of nervousness and pain, but for staying awake nothing better has ever been invented. The small country, for example, expects its people to be ecstatic about the sacrifices that will lead it to its new bed, expects that the large country will welcome its coming of age and even lend it some pillows. Éliane expects a fundamental upheaval if she obeys Nick Rosenfeld's insistent siren call to return to him. *(Are we going to let THIS die?)* What will happen if he says, *"I love you,"* terrifying cinematic words that lead to an abyss? What will happen if he doesn't say them? What will happen to the small country if it can't convince anyone? It's time to stop being afraid. It's time to find out.

Nothing is easier than slipping from the small country to the large one, nothing is more mechanically done. You take the airplane along with the business people with their briefcases stuffed with statistics. An hour and a half later you land and you're with Nick Rosenfeld.

Éliane had forgotten that Nick Rosenfeld is as big and cold as an Arctic landscape. Sunglasses hide his eyes. In the car from the airport he drives quickly and speaks reservedly. Éliane is frozen with dread until suddenly, at a stoplight, Nick Rosenfeld takes her hand and crushes it in his own. Almost immediately after they arrive at his house he relieves her of her suitcase, her hesitations, her clothes, and the magic begins again—his cool greedy mouth on her as on a Stradivarius, the ardent music of his voice. *(Oh you. Éliane. Oh my dear. My love.)*

They make love all through the day, the evening—eight times in a row, Éliane marvels silently when in a moment of calm she regains the ability to count. They make short work of the foie gras and champagne that Éliane brought; Nick Rosenfeld's triumphant hedonism is entirely concentrated elsewhere. *(You're so sexy. You're so. Oh you.)* Late in the evening, his legs still imprisoned by Éliane's, he stretches out his arm and plays with the television remote control for a moment. The usual world, a world suddenly extraordinarily strange, fills up the screen: what are all those dressed and anxious people doing there? Why are they discussing things so painfully instead of caressing each other? Éliane props herself up on an elbow when she recognizes Filippo. The small country is speaking, on tape. Seen from here, between foreign sheets wet with pleasure, the small country seems so sad and pathetic. Filippo's face is that of an exhausted knight questing after a constantly fleeing Holy Grail. From here, between crumpled sheets untouched by fear, you can see that the small country's quest is a terrible trial. How can it be cut short, prevented from going on for ever? Oh, the small country's distress is so obvious, it would so like to be strong and sure of itself, would so like to stop being afraid of its own disappearance. Éliane asks Nick Rosenfeld to turn off the television.

Nick Rosenfeld is prey to a mysterious alternation. On his feet, he becomes stiff and locked into formal declarations. *(We get along so well. I am sure we will be friends.)* Lying down, he burns like a volcano with an inexhaustible supply of lava. *(Oh Éliane. Oh lovely. Oh you. You.)* All these hours spent dwelling inside each other are terribly explosive. But since it is absolutely necessary to stand up to get anywhere, it is the vertical and glacial Nick Rosenfeld who drives Éliane back to the airport. Through which wounds, which invisible holes, does he lose his heat so suddenly? Better not to dwell on questions that have no answers. Better to pick up a newspaper to escape the inexplicable. The inexplicable is also found in the airplane newspapers. In these papers, published by the large country, it is written that the small country isn't a country. It is written that there is nothing distinctive about the small country, nothing to preserve, nothing to demand. If it changes beds, we'll make sleep impossible. Why is the small country, which is made up of everything that defines a country, not a country?

The large country's journalists don't say. Another question given up without an answer, more that's inexplicable to be escaped.

Coming home, the thing to do would be to go back to the computer and the familiar walls as though nothing had happened. Maybe nothing has happened, since Filippo senses no new odour on Éliane. The odours are hidden inside, along with Nick Rosenfeld's hot horizontal voice, and that secret entity paws and snorts as it hunts for a way out.

Is it possible to be in love with the memory of a voice and a mouth, obsessed by what we know is only a mirage that will leave us even thirstier than before if we persist in going back? It seems so. Éliane knows the cold parts of Nick Rosenfeld and the scantiness of their common ground. She also sees that the meeting of their bodies has eliminated that of their minds: since the time Nick Rosenfeld's mouth broke a dike in her, they've never again talked about the large country and the small country, they've never again talked about anything rational or professional. Nonetheless, she would like to reconstitute the whole, starting with the torrid parts of Nick Rosenfeld—as though the cold parts hadn't already won the battle. Nick Rosenfeld has rejected her, since he no longer calls her.

The most painful death is by rejection. There are times in front of the television when Filippo and Éliane don't speak. When they hear the testimonies of people who've come from elsewhere but who have lived here for a long time and still deny the existence of the small country in which they are comfortably settled, Filippo and Éliane are gripped by a pain that crushes the words in their mouths. The words don't exist to condemn these people from outside, these decent friendly people who reject their hosts' right to survive. Filippo and Éliane have both worked so hard to see things from these others' points of view that they even understand the complex motivations for this rejection. But the pain remains, overwhelming; how can they bear it that the others never, in turn, try to see things through their eyes?

Éliane decides to write to Nick Rosenfeld. She wants to know what that essential thing was—that thing whose very existence was at stake—that made it necessary for her to come back to him *(Are we going to let THIS die?)* and then came to an end before she could see it bloom. It's not easy to put into words. Once again she has to fight on his ground, to probe the foreign words from every angle to get at their soul. As an exercise, Éliane translates everything she hears into Nick Rosenfeld's language. *Pass me the butter. Give me a break. Do you agree with the law voted by the National Assembly and proclaiming a new bed? Yes or No.* She translates the consultations that are taped and rebroadcast on television in the evenings. Sometimes she doesn't need to translate, because the speeches are already in his language: for example, those by the First Nations chiefs, wrapped in the dignity of their own tragic extinction, who come to oppose the survival of the small country. That leaves only Filippo to translate, Filippo's imperturbable questions: *"What do you mean when you say that we are not a nation?"* But mentally translating Filippo is a difficult experience, it leaves her terribly ashamed. That's the moment when she feels that she is truly betraying him, that she's betraying him a lot more than with Nick Rosenfeld.

In the end, Éliane doesn't need to write Nick Rosenfeld, because the answer to the question she can't put into words is suddenly everywhere around her. She has only to say his name in a vaguely detached tone; an amazing number of people she knows know Nick Rosenfeld, or rather, know a number of women who have shared Nick Rosenfeld's horizontal fevers. It seems that any woman who moves into the range of his cold eye finds herself aflame in Nick Rosenfeld's bed, in a fleeting passion that has little to do with her.

We understand everything about people and nations when we understand the nature of their quest. Nick Rosenfeld's quest is dreamlike and abstract. It goes far beyond Éliane, far beyond real women. Nick Rosenfeld's quest demands that he lie down with them right away, with his eyes closed, the better to escape them. Now Éliane understands. The hardest thing is to understand that Nick Rosenfeld's special music— the music she found so moving— had nothing to do with her personally. *(Oh Éliane. Oh Carole. Oh Teresa. My love. Oh you.)*

The small country's quest, by contrast, has a real destination, even if a long-delayed one. But now, after all these preliminaries, the moment of truth has arrived. The Final Consultation with the small country's insomnia-stunned citizens is taking place. Where will they finally sleep?

When the verdict comes down, Filippo and Éliane are inside the television set. They are participating in a special program on the Final Consultation. Like the other guests, they make measured comments, and to react to the situation calmly they choose the most roundabout words. It's not until much later, on the living-room sofa, that their feelings send them into each other's arms.

It's a sharp pain, a disappointment so violent it could turn to hatred. Hatred, yes, that would be easy, and maybe a consolation. Éliane and Filippo are tempted by hatred for their fellow citizens, hatred for those parts of themselves that have turned cowardly for fear of being fanatical. Brave sheep. Then the hatred blurs, because it doesn't make anything better. Half of the small country's people are afraid to live in an unknown bed. The other half are afraid of dying in the old familiar one. How can you tell which of these two fears is the most worthy?

Should a metaphorical relationship be seen between

Éliane's disappointment in love and the ideological disappointment of the small country? I personally would distrust that, like anything that is too easy. Yes, Nick Rosenfeld belongs to the big country whose suffocating embrace Éliane fears. But life is full of circumstantial hazards, and a woman is not a country, no matter how small.

Despite everything, the end of the story comes from Nick Rosenfeld. He telephones Éliane the day after the Final Consultation. *(Hello, Éliane. It's Nick Rosenfeld.)* And while she is stiff with mistrust, and doesn't speak, he says these few words, the most tender she has heard in his language, he just repeats these few truly soothing words. *(I'm sorry. I'm sorry.)*

FRANCOPHONIE

FOR *Patrick Cady*

N I C O L A S   T O C Q U E V I L L E arrived from Paris, eyes alert and glowing despite the time difference, his intellectual's grey hair flowing down his neck, his three-piece suit just wrinkled enough to give his otherwise elegantly trendy appearance a delinquent charm. He had the vigorous fiftyish air of those unburdened by useless regrets, and the various women he favoured with a smile while passing through the restaurant were quick to return it. Sylvain Duchesne, weak-kneed with emotion, nevertheless managed to get up from the table to greet him. Warmly they crushed hands and exchanged their names like cabbalistic passwords.

This meeting was out of the ordinary. Three months before, Sylvain had received a letter from Paris, from the prestigious publishing house of Galligrasseuil. He had not solicited anything from them, the letter was in reply to nothing at all, as free as a miracle. For three amazing pages Nicolas Tocqueville, the literary director, analysed and praised Sylvain's books, even though they were distributed only in Quebec; he pushed his admirable empathy to the point of proposing that they meet the next time his job brought him to Montreal.

Since then, Sylvain had been severely shaken. Understand that Sylvain dared presume to write and publish essays in this paranoiac and adolescent country where televised sagas are still believed to constitute the quintessence of literature, in this comical country which seems more terrified of its tiny intellectual elite than of its numerous crapulous gangsters. Essays, alas. Why not elegies in ancient Greek or vernacular Latin, the miserable social misfit? He had certainly received eulogistic reviews and a literary prize, but he'd never succeeded in reaching more than five hundred readers, and although he pretended not to care it hurt him terribly, and his hurt had gradually evolved into something more acrid, more purulent, as do all secret wounds.

But now Nicolas Tocqueville, the living balm, was sitting across from him and, in his healing voice, ordering oysters, marinated salmon, a very rare entrecôte béarnaise and wine. It was almost enough to bring tears to Sylvain's eyes. Finally a real Frenchman, someone still joyfully epicurean despite the now compulsory fitness—a suicide with style, if staying alive means nibbling at vitaminized vegetables and washing them down with mineral water. Nicolas Tocqueville even lit up a Gitane, and slowly blew its smoke towards the anti-smoking notice pinned to the wall.

He sighed, "I'm so happy to be here with you, Sylvain. What an incredible country, on the fifteenth of November it's already snowing. Tell me about yourself. Sovereignty has become inevitable, hasn't it?"

Sylvain made a discreet face. Of course they would have to dissect all the ins and outs of Quebec, they would have to weigh the consequences and the surprises of the latest penultimate referendum, they would have to have an endless discussion about the future of a people made up of such disparate elements that we have to keep redefining it. But the later the better, and Sylvain even tried to put it off for ever.

"Did you know," he asked, as though joking, "that in this incredible, as you call it, country, the word 'intellectual' is an insult?"

For a moment, Nicolas Tocqueville held his mouth half open beside an oyster already harpooned and just waiting to be consumed; then he swallowed it with a smile.

"You almost amaze me," he said.

Then he began to talk, and he continued right through the meal, so much so that he might have been unable to both express his opinions and retain the juices of his considerable portions of food had he not had the unusual ability to move his uvula and tongue alternately in such a way that he could swallow and speak at the same time. As for Sylvain, he hardly touched his food, since he couldn't be hungry and shocked at the same time.

Yes, he was shocked. Nothing is more shocking than hearing someone talk about you, than seeing yourself larger than life in someone else's eyes, nothing is more difficult than hearing compliments and making a suitable face, one reflecting something between false modesty and swollen pride.

Not only had Nicolas Tocqueville ploughed through Sylvain's work, right down to its most subterranean roots, gotten hold of the last unfindable copies of *On All Fours* and *Sitting Down*, gone through the difficult *Kneeling* and sardonic *Lying Down* from cover to cover, but he had unearthed illuminations that no Quebec critic had had the energy or talent to unearth before, constructed complex interpretations that Sylvain would never have imagined possible, even perceived in Sylvain a surprising cultural interbreeding with the North American Indians, and he delivered all this in a lump to the party concerned, who had become as speechless and red as a theatre janitor who suddenly finds himself in the spotlight. Nicolas Tocqueville ended on the subject of Quebec, the apparent non-intellectualism of Quebec, "a definitive proof of health and democracy, do you understand, Sylvain?" he hammered at Sylvain, who wanted only to understand, "the proof that you haven't broken with your origins the disastrous way we in France have done," he concluded, while wreathing the stoical waiter who had arrived to clear the table in a thick cloud of smoke.

A silence settled between them, a silence that was like a vibrant continuation of what had been said, a digestive pause to allow a breathing space for this marvellous beginning to a friendship. Sylvain surprised himself by calmly waiting for what was coming, anticipating the blessed outline in advance. Now the esteemed director of Galligrasseuil was going to get down to concrete details, and Sylvain was ready. (Yes, since you mention it, I'm just doing the last revisions on the final version of my next essay, *Standing Up*, a five-hundred-page sociopsychoanalytic analysis of the suicidal inertia of the Quebec educational system, and yes, I do envisage eventually publishing with you, once, of course, we've agreed on the size of the print run and certain conditions of publication that, what can you do, my rigorous sense of ethics condemns me to insist on—where do I sign?...)

But Nicolas Tocqueville continued his tribute, this time including numerous other Quebec writers, including some whose genius was very highly debatable by Sylvain's stringent criteria—and Sylvain, swallowing his arrogance, became suddenly suspicious.

"But Mr. Tocqueville, you're not going to tell me you've found the time to read every writer in Montreal?" he tried to joke.

Or to write them personally, he didn't dare add, gripped by a small sadness.

"Call me Tocque, that's what my friends call me," Nicolas Tocqueville said.

He gave Sylvain such a wide smile that a couple of decayed premolars suddenly became visible.

"I've read you all," he said. "Tomorrow I'm meeting Denis Fafouin, the poet, and the novelist Pamela Ducharme—are they friends of yours? So wonderfully insolent, so fresh!"

For a few minutes Sylvain was intensely disappointed. To find himself one of a crowd in Nicolas Tocqueville's known as Tocque's heart definitely reduced the magic. Too bad. In this unbearable country the collective destiny could not be escaped, writers were condemned never to be able to save themselves individually, their shoulders were harnessed to the yoke of solidarity, their feet entangled in fleurs-de-lis.

Meanwhile, the customers around them had become noisy and frantic—no doubt chemically overexcited by the imminent Montreal snowstorm. We are dogs, Sylvain thought sadly, we are ruled by our instincts like dogs. Nicolas Tocqueville, a round wine stain on his fine silk shirt, had shifted his chair in a way that enabled him to see the whole restaurant and tenderly contemplate the spectacle of these overexcited instincts. Sylvain was ashamed of his disappointment. Finally, someone from over there had allowed himself to be deeply interested in the culture of here. How dare he not be happy about it? Finally Paris, so brilliant and so condescending, was coming close enough to Montreal to discover a sexy foreigner instead of a poor cousin, and was kissing it on the mouth.

The second meeting between Sylvain Duchesne and Nicolas Tocqueville took place two months later, in the midst of a snowy winter which had by that time evolved into a permanent catastrophe. For the occasion Sylvain had invited some lovers of fine writing and alcohol to his house, and his wife, Christine, had decided to make Beef Wellington. Very rare, at Sylvain's request.

Besides Denis Fafouin and Pamela Ducharme, there was the very young novelist Luc Sylvestre, the less-young novelist

Dominique Larue, John Sedgewick, who was a poet-musician, and the inflammatory playwright Betsi Larousse. All these intelligences whose reputations were fundamentally confined to their own country had had the right to a letter from Nicolas Tocqueville and the nectar of his praises. No doubt they too had silently digested the disappointment of not being unique. Now, profiting from the lateness of the one who had lyrically expressed his love to them, they were discussing the event with the help of olives and whiskey.

Two opposing camps were gradually being formed: those who were flattered and found it wonderful to have been found wonderful, and those who were angry at themselves for feeling flattered and wanted more. Sylvain was in the first group. Denis Fafouin was a savage proponent of the second.

"I don't understand you," Sylvain was saying. "After all, nothing forced this man to come here and tell us we're good."

"If we're so good as all that," sneered Denis Fafouin, "why hasn't Galligrasseuil ever published a single one of our books?"

"Personally, I've never sent them a manuscript," Betsi Larousse lied.

"I did," said Pamela Ducharme in her velvet voice. "My books have been co-published with our brother Tocque twice."

"And?"

"And nothing," she continued smiling. "Both times my books were displayed for half an hour in Paris bookstores before being put back in their cartons."

"Aha!" Denis Fafouin exclaimed triumphantly.

"Aha what?" Sylvain asked, irritated. "What does that prove?"

"It proves France is closed as tight as a clam, and finds us as interesting as a piece of dog poo."

"But who gives a fuck about France?" Luc Sylvestre grumbled over his third whiskey, and the others considered him with the sardonic smile reserved for the very young who don't yet know what's important in this life.

Because if there was a consensus among the Francophone intellectual community on this side of the Atlantic, it was this: we did give a fuck about France, if only to retain a bit of balance in this disturbing period when there was no lack of neighbours happy to offer us a friendly push towards oblivion.

"Anyway," concluded Dominique Larue, who spoke rarely but always to the point, "he is the literary director, he is from Paris, he does respect us, let's wait until he spits it out."

Two hours later, Nicolas Tocqueville landed at Sylvain's door. He had come from Europe the same day, as always unaffected by the time change, his colouring sharpened by the cold air, his hair whitened by the snow, as enthusiastic as a liberated schoolboy. He slipped into the group and their renewed passions with a chameleon's grace and soon even his laughter took on the same drunken timbre as the others. The only tiny mistake he made was when he insisted, as a hopelessly stupid Parisian romantic, on the psychic similarities between Quebeckers and American Indians, going so far as a detailed psychoanalytic theory about the "Brébeuf complex," which supposedly incited the first Canadian martyrs to seek out torture in order to better identify with the Iroquois warriors.

"All right," Sylvain quickly forestalled him, "let's continue the debate over the 'Bréboeuf' Wellington."

Vast quantities were eaten and drunk, John Sedgewick caterwauled through his saxophone, Denis Fafouin improvised hilarious haiku about sex and death and, most of all, they played the very favourite game of this country's intellectuals, the self-demolition game.

This was a strange game that left the players more despairing than diverted, and consisted of tirelessly flagellating the defects of their own society until, bled dry, it collapsed. There were no winners in this cruel game, except for an abstract utopian purity, the purity of ideas carried to the point of suicide. Perhaps that was what made the exercise fascinating.

Sylvain excelled at it, he was the one who began with savage sarcasms about the Minister of Education, more swine than swineherd, followed by an implacable assassination of the entire educational system, a fiasco which had irremediably plunged the country into obscurantism (besides, this was the theme of his forthcoming book, *Standing Up*, which he hoped universities would put on their compulsory reading list). The others leapt gaily into the arena and machine-gunned all the fleur-de-lis-shaped things they could find—a society of drawers of water, a people given over to the worship of servility and hockey players, a small-minded nation drifting into triumphant xenophobia, horrible little Quebec.

Nicolas Tocqueville listened to all this with an unbelieving smile, then suddenly put an energetic stop to The Game.

"Allow me," he said, "allow an outside observer to express his disagreement."

Never, he assured them, never had he encountered such contemptuous self-criticism and such aggressive watchdogs as in this small country, this small young country which was nevertheless infinitely more tolerant and courageous than any other to which his thrilling life had led him. "What are you trying to prove by hating yourselves this way?" he asked them, looking them right in the eye. "What are you after, Sylvain, Denis, Pamela, Luc, Betsi, Dominique, Christine, John?"

There was a silence. Sylvain crouched on the floor, Pamela began to weep silently and none of them knew how to respond, because the truth was that this small country they were cutting up so resentfully was what they loved most in the world; this small country that kept disappearing on them made them so sad that to protect themselves they had to pretend to despise it.

The third meeting between Sylvain Duchesne and Nicolas Tocqueville took place at Mirabel Airport.

Something decisive had quietly made its way through Sylvain, sending a raw shaft of light to his convoluted brain.

He was going to move to Paris.

He would move to Paris to serve Montreal better, he would be the essential link ensuring that literature from here was implanted there, and Nicolas Tocqueville, who didn't yet know it, would help by providing a door—a trap door would do—into the sleek publishing house of Galligrasseuil.

Our brother Tocque was, to tell the truth, taking a long time to "spit it out," to repeat Dominique Larue's cavalier words, but he was keeping up an assiduous correspondence with Sylvain in which his adulation of Quebec remained firm, this Quebec so vital compared to ossified Paris, as he never stopped saying.

It was time to prod him to pass from words to deeds.

For his part, Sylvain was more than ready to exchange, at least temporarily, the convulsive coughing of Quebec for the wonderful ossification of Paris. Temporarily, beginning any time.

In fact, since he'd put the finishing touches on his manuscript *Standing Up*, he had been unable to stay in one spot, he slept poorly, his mind wasn't on his teaching, he was no longer here, he could only picture himself over there, rue de Rennes in the *sixième*, ecstatically ensconced in a Galligrasseuil cubbyhole, his Mont Blanc in a frenzy as he annotated manuscripts from Quebec—excuse me, from the Francophones of the Americas—before bringing them into the big adjoining office, the beloved office of the beloved Tocque, who was just waiting for him to give the green light so he could publish them.

From a distance, it seemed to him, he too would find a fresh point of view from which to admire the untamed panorama of his homeland, his so-timid homeland which for the moment he had to admit, he was finding ever more depressing.

Sylvain didn't tell anyone his plan—not his writer friends, not Nicolas Tocqueville, not even his wife, Christine. Are we not alone when we die and when we are born, when we die in our old life to be reincarnated in a new one?

One morning he stuffed his manuscript *Standing Up* into a suitcase, along with a few clothes, and decided to go to Paris to prepare the ground. Without warning he would lay siege to Galligrasseuil, push open all the doors, squat in Tocque's office until his initiative was applauded.

He got to Mirabel very early, as he couldn't help doing before important trips. Sufficiently early to see, arriving in the middle of the airport, tousled, excited by the Arctic light and the American vastness, the passengers from Paris. Among them, dragging a mound of suitcases in his elegant wake, was Nicolas Tocqueville.

They saw each other at the same time and lifted their arms to wave in perfect synchronicity, Sylvain amazed, Nicolas Tocqueville overjoyed.

"I'm coming to stay!" Tocque called across to him. "I'm coming to stay, Sylvain!"

"You're what?" Sylvain called back, trying to extricate himself from the lineup.

"I've just said to hell with it all!...Fuck Paris! Fuck Galligrasseuil! I'm coming to stay, *tabernacle!*"

And that was all he could say before he was swallowed up by the customs officials who were clearing his passage to the New World.

RED AND WHITE

I'M NOT going to kill myself any more. I am saying this to you, Aataentsic, mother of humanity who made the earth and tends its souls, from now on I will live as long as life is willing to stay in me, I will learn to stroke my anger and my hatred until they grow dull as inoffensive mice.

Already I, who never used to talk, have found the words to convince the doctor to let me leave. I only needed a few, but I needed to choose them quickly from among those they know how to understand here. I said I was going back to Kanahwake, where my own people were waiting for me, I said that where I lived there were healing circles that were much more powerful than all his anti-depressants. Then I apologized for my rudeness, all the while looking him in the eyes the way they do here, so immodestly. When this doctor whose hair had gone white with something other than wisdom finally asked me why I had wanted to die, I said with a straight face that I'd been unhappy in love. That was the answer and the image he was hoping for, the universal image of a young woman mistreated by love rather than that of an ageless savage ravaged by hate.

I'd never had any victories so I thought it would be exhilarating to win. But he was so easily conquered that I felt more embarrassed than proud.

Leaving the hospital I looked at the sun, calmly shining, warm and alive despite everything it has seen. For the first time I knew that I was twenty-five years old and that hate is no way to survive.

I'm not going back to Kanahwake. I'm staying here in Montreal, in this old Hochelaga where my ancestors lived huddled into the mountainsides. I have decided to infiltrate those who keep on conquering us.

I want to see us the way they see us. I want to put their cold eyes into my own to see what we've become, without blinking or breaking down.

O Aataentsic, our mother, we have become homeless wanderers. We are without shelter in our humiliating reserves, and the spirit that made us strong now bleeds out of us, drop by drop, exhausted. We are poor among the poor, tethered like unloved livestock to bits of rock, when we get thirsty, all we can do is drink. Flushed with shame, we beg for casinos, for the right to smuggle, for money, for things that deaden the mind and wither the soul. Our warriors have become so weak that they beat their wives instead of mastering their fears. We watch television to see the suffering of our faraway brothers in Davis Inlet, in Goose Bay, in Calgary, we watch television to dream of being cowboys instead of Indians. We display our humiliation everywhere, a humiliation that kills, but so slowly that no sees it any more.

I want to see with their eyes how they end up condemning us instead of pitying us.

It's true that they are the conquerors and that we are enemies. Our parallel paths have been forced to intersect, and neither they nor we will ever be happy about that. Like water and flame, we are enemies: this is a thought that never leaves me, even when I'm sitting beside them in their buses and their subways, when I buy their meat or smile at those among them who are the least indifferent.

I want to taste the salt of their tears when they weep about the injustices they've suffered these last hundred years yet forget ours, which have lasted for centuries. I want to listen to their radio talk shows and read their newspapers. I want to absorb all their speeches in order to assess their animosity and their weaknesses. I want to learn to talk quickly and loudly the way they do, crushing opposing arguments in advance. I want to contemplate them, prisoners of the mirage of their bodies and their worldly goods, gliding above the emptiness that has replaced their souls.

I want to understand why they conquered us.

When I return to my own people, I will have their strength in addition to my own, and maybe this time I'll be able to watch the children of Davis Inlet sniffing glue without killing myself.

The time has come to have a warrior's heart, hardened by purity and vigilance, armed with the strength of nature instead of things that kill. We will not survive in their earth-defiling furrows, where every seed sown becomes violence and egotism, we will not survive without rediscovering our own path. They are part of the most important battle we have ever faced. The most important battle we have ever faced is taking place with them at our sides, like a granite wall against which our hands bleed in desperation. Never has the danger been so great, never in our long struggle to survive wolverines, famine, freezing cold, enemies with weapons more powerful and ruthless than our own. The time has come to confront time itself, to adapt to a life whose face has changed. There is nowhere to escape to. This noisy earth with its garrulous inhabitants and treeless forests is all that's left to us; we must put down new roots or accept death.

That's why I'm praying to you this evening, Aataentsic, our faceless mother in whom I stopped believing long ago. This evening, my prayer makes you exist, and tears that flow from my eyes aren't tears of weakness but the tears of renewal. Above my bed I've hung the Mohawk dream-catcher my father left me, made of bear skulls and eagle feathers more powerful than sleeping pills. It will take every magic there is to get me through the coming nights without nightmares. But there are so many days between the nights, so many days when I must stay upright in their Montreal, and tame my anger and overcome the obstacles.

Help me, O Aataentsic, to remain a human being.

IT

IT'S LYING down on the sidewalk. It might be a sculpture. Off-off-ex-post-modern. Go closer. Up close it stinks, it stinks and, no, it moves and it has eyes. It has a large green bag overflowing with things. Let's see what's in the bag. It complains a bit when we take it away, luckily it doesn't bite. We open the bag.

An empty Caribou bottle falls out, along with some Canadian Tire money, a torn hockey sweater, an expired STCUM card, a piece of the Olympic Stadium, a shred of the distinct society and an old picture, a picture of it when it was small and human and dreamed of becoming an astronaut.

FUCKING BOURGEOIS

I could hear the human noise
we made there sitting,
not one of us moving,
not even when the room went dark.

Raymond Carver
What We Talk about When
We Talk about Love

THE TUNA smells of fresh almond. I don't resist the desire to cut myself a thick strip and eat it like that, raw, without anything, in its naked perfection. It's so good it makes the eyes close and inspires meditation. In the distance I can hear the depressing sound of the news and I know that Thomas is in front of the television, his eyes open wide so he won't miss a detail of the live broadcast of the universe's collapse. Afterwards, to shake off the inevitable bad mood, he'll have to be told witty stories, given a drink, kissed behind the ear in that scented and ticklish zone where he's still a little boy. I cut the tuna into fillets, spread it out in the lemon slices, oil, pink peppercorns and tarragon. I plunge the marrowbone into salted boiling water. I cut the carrots and zucchini into round slices. All these precise actions give immediate results and odours: food never lets you down, if you treat it with love.

Thomas comes back into the kitchen, burdened by what burdens humanity. He tells me all of it. People are killing each other all over the place because of gods and fences, children are smoking crack instead of playing dodgeball, men are beating women who have slipped their leashes. And in the heart of our own so-civilized home behind the Place des Arts, there is a human being sleeping outside at twenty-five degrees below zero.

"You know," Thomas says, "last night, with the wind, it went down to thirty below. A woman almost sixty years old, arse-deep in the snow under newspapers and plastic bags, waiting for sunrise, and what a sun, it's intolerable. Intolerable."

While he's speaking, the marrow comes out of the bone with an oily gurgle—and I see the woman, her wrecked face stunned and blotchy. Sleeping under the snow like a piece of anonymous detritus, then waking up in front of the news cameras, the shock of it, the shock and the fabulous dramatic situation. The marrow has to be cut into manageable strips before it congeals. I have to get Thomas a drink. The woman and her Kafkaesque awakening must be kept in mind for later, for tomorrow, when it's time to invent fictions more real than reality. ("It's not the cold and the need for alcohol that pull her from her sleep on this morning, but a tall boy calling 'Cut!' behind a blinding sun—another nightmare, she says to herself, a day nightmare, which is the worst kind.")

I set the appetizers out on the white china to enhance their contrasting colours: grilled pistachios, olives with anchovies, marinated chanterelles and pholiotes for Jean-Eudes, who likes mushrooms, sweetbread mousse on toast for Lili, who likes everything. Oh, the warm welcoming evening that lies ahead of us, the pleasure of giving and taking, the miracle of friendship.

"All this fuss just for Lili," Thomas says.

He goes to set the table and I can hear the plates clattering. When he comes back into the kitchen I take hold of the back of his silk shirt, the one that makes him look like a Venetian painter, and he calms down and allows himself to be kissed.

The telephone rings, let them not be the ones that something regrettable has happened to. Thomas answers. He says, "Just a moment." Then he says, "It's for you."

At the other end of the line the woman's voice is far away, it's the transatlantic kind that disturbs intimate Saturday evenings. It's just an invitation to take part in a conference, nothing could be easier to decline and get rid of quickly.

There's still time to cut the mango into pieces, lick the musky juice from my fingers. Take the beef filets from the refrigerator, sample a stray morsel. Rearrange the mimosa on the table.

"A conference? Where?" Thomas asks.

"In Casablanca."

"Casablanca," he repeats.

His eyes haven't moved from the spot near the table where I'm no longer standing. Even when Lili and Jean-Eudes ring the doorbell, he doesn't move. Until I call, "Thomas?" Then he looks up towards the door, he rushes to open it, makes a few inaudible jokes, and I hear Lili's laugh tumbling down to me as if from a Russian mountain.

They've brought flowers, wine, Belgian chocolates. "The chocolates are just for you," Lili says. "I forbid you to offer any to Thomas, that pig." Jean-Eudes sniffs my neck: "It's the same perfume you wore in school," he says, and Lili rolls her eyes towards the ceiling, as she often does when he opens his mouth. Thomas puts on some blues and makes margaritas, Lili and I stretch out languidly on the floor, continuing to pretend it's summer.

"I could kill someone," Lili says. "Pass me those sweetbread things and I'll murder them instead. I'm going to put on another five pounds tonight, you bitch, Claire."

She's been to interview Rhapsode, the singer who sold a hundred thousand copies of her hit "Tickle Me" and is preparing to record it in Japanese. "I suggested another, more Asiatic title to her," Lili snickers, "Scratch Me Low."

"Scratch my noh," Thomas corrects, and here we are laughing like idiots already, the tequila fumes in our brains.

"I just can't do it any more," says Lili, "I've got showbiz and success stories coming out of my ears, what's in these olives? I'd sell my mother for these. Nothing more depressing than interviewing a rising singer, nothing more monotonous, what's their dream, all of them, from the very depths of their deepest self, what's the craziest and most poetic dream, those giant navel-gazers, what do you think?—it's to be on the Johnny Carson show one day. It's to be known in the United States, the world centre of bad taste."

"Not all of them," Thomas says. "The proof is Rhapsode—she's dreaming of Japan."

"It's the same," Lili says. "Japan, the States, the lowest common denominator."

"When we make something, love," Jean-Eudes says, "don't you think it's normal to want it to be seen by as many people as possible?"

"No," Lili says.

"Come on," Jean-Eudes says, "you, a journalist who lives for the size of your print runs and prime time..."

"Exactly," Lili says. "I'm sick of it. Stop trying to trap me, you're bugging me."

"I'm not trapping you, love, we're having a discussion," Jean-Eudes says.

He touches her hair furtively from behind. She puts her head back and drinks, she closes her eyes and she hums, *Nobody knows you when you're down and out.*

"Eric Clapton," she says. "I'd like to hear Eric Clapton."

The glasses are almost empty now. I push the marinated mushrooms towards Jean-Eudes, the olives towards Lili, get up and look through the compact discs.

"Relax, Claire," Lili says.

"Let it flop," Thomas says. "That's what the pupils tell me when I ask them questions. Or a variation: relax your shaft. There's one student who always takes out his knife when I start my class. A jack-knife. He carves up his desk while he watches me."

"Come on," Jean-Eudes says, "aren't weapons forbidden in the schools?"

"Yes," Thomas says.

Lili watches, smiling.

"Nasty job you've got," she says.

"You said it," Thomas says.

"When you think that when I was twenty," Lili says, "I wanted to be Oriana Fallaci, do in-depth investigations that would blow people's minds. But how can you do great work here? There are no stakes, there's no cause. Quibbles over billboards, speeches about budgets and cutbacks, that's what delights and occupies us, we've become a nation of accountants."

I pour the rest of the margarita mix into their three glasses, collect the empty plates.

"Do you need some help?" Jean-Eudes asks.

I tell him to stay sitting down and let it flop. He laughs, a hiccuping juvenile laugh that follows me to the kitchen and takes me back to our schooldays, when we both did theatre and he was never able to stay serious.

I prepare four beds of radicchio on which I lay the tuna. Onto each strip of tuna goes a sprig of fennel, a few pink peppercorns. I cut the bread. From the refrigerator I take out the foie gras, the cheese, a bottle of white—a 1983 Sancerre whose fruity taste will resist the fish marinade. I light the oven and set it to 375 degrees. Taking my time, I remove the foie gras from its mould, enjoying the feel of this smooth, glistening miracle that smells of contraband and sin.

They're still talking about work in the living-room, while Eric Clapton scoffs: *Before you accuse me, take a look at yerself....* Lili rolls a joint.

"I don't agree," Jean-Eudes is saying. "For ten years I've been making maps for the city and I still like it, I like my job."

"You," Lili says, without raising her eyes from her grass, "you're something else. You have so little anger," she adds, after a pause, looking him in the eyes.

"Claire's the one with the job," Thomas says. "She works here quietly, without anyone to bug her, she tells herself stories that everyone buys."

"It's true that Claire is lucky," Lili says, smiling at me.

"Today," Thomas says, taking me by the hand to force me to sit next to him, "she was invited to Casablanca and she said no, my dear, she said no and she doesn't even talk to me about it, as if nothing is more ordinary than being invited to Casablanca and saying, no thank you."

"Casablanca," Lili says.

I try to justify myself, I get confused, what do they all think is so great about Casablanca? I'm behind in my work, I no more have time to go to Casablanca than to go to Ouarjetou.

"That's my sweetie," Thomas says, squeezing my hand too hard, "that's how she is, admired and modest."

"To Claire," Lili says, lifting her glass, which still has a few drops of alcohol.

"To Claire," Thomas and Jean-Eudes say.

I would like to propose a toast to love and friendship, but the words are hesitant coming out, ridiculous and stiff, so I say, "To you!" raising my empty glass, and at that moment I know how much I love them, they are the people I love most in the world.

At first the tuna carpaccio is eaten in silence, during the time it takes for the delicate ocean fragrance to settle on the amazed taste-buds. Thomas pours the wine. Lili gives a long sigh.

"Delicious," she groans.

"How did you meet each other?" Jean-Eudes asks. "I don't remember."

"Really?" Thomas says. "You don't remember?"

He gives me a mocking look and stops speaking, it's up to me to tell the story. I say, "We met eight years ago. At a literary event. Afterwards I invited him to my place."

Thomas gives a long laugh, as though at a hilarious riposte. Lili lights her joint. She inhales and lets it burn between her fingers. Jean-Eudes holds out his hand so she'll pass it to him, but she keeps it, a sphinx-like half-smile on her lips.

"My dear Claire," Thomas laughs. "That 'literary event,' as she puts it so remarkably succinctly, was the time Claire got the Prix Réjean-Ducharme, winning easily over the other competitors, who didn't even come close. I was one of them."

"What do you mean?" Jean-Eudes asks. "You were what?"

"I was a competitor, a nominee, a finalist, a poor scribbler that the stupid jury had put on the list for this stupid prize, what's going on, Jean-Eudes, don't you listen when people speak to you?"

"Ah," Jean-Eudes says, taking a puff of grass, "I didn't know you write."

"I don't write any more, I'm a teacher, a dull-witted teacher unable to relax my shaft. Once, when I was younger, I wrote a book, it was a bad idea, the book stank, books should be left to those who know how to write them, like Claire."

It doesn't do any good to protest but I do anyway, while Thomas smokes without looking at me. I say the same things that I always say and that always fall flat—but Thomas, your book was good, the proof is that the jury chose it...

"A dirty trick," Thomas says, "and you know it very well, but it's not important. Claire was charming, she made a very humble speech and I came up to congratulate her and we had a drink together, and afterwards I went to her place and the most amazing thing was that she also had style in bed, you have to admit that isn't so easy."

Perhaps to slow them down I should open a red instead of another white. Perhaps I should have put more on the plates, the tuna disappeared more quickly than when it was hooked, but no, still to come are the generous helpings of beef filet, the Buron cheeses, the salad, the clementine sorbet served in the peel, the truffles from Le Nôtre.

I turn on the heat for the steamed vegetables. The tournedos are sizzling in butter and oil, I turn them quickly so they stay very rare, a bit of salt, pepper, and now they're onto a platter, each one with a slice of foie gras mashed onto it so the pâté will stick to the meat, topped with a few slices of marrow, they are already giving off irresistible odours. I add enough flour to the pan juices to make a roux, then I put in some port, bouillon, a bit of marrow to make the mixture smoother.

"That smells good," Jean-Eudes says behind me. "Can I help?"

He carries the dinner plates like a precious cargo, unsure of finding a safe destination. I take them from him and he sits down, relieved.

"It'll be three years for us. It was here that you introduced us, wasn't it? No, it was at L'Express. Three years. I'd like to organize a party in honour of that, three years is something to celebrate, it seems to me, a big party without telling her about it, you know how Lili is, how she hates anniversaries. They say it's a critical milestone, three years, I don't know why, I love her more than I used to, more and more all the time, it's crazy."

His pupils are dilated by the grass and by something sad and elusive that's trying to emerge. Words come to me that aren't for him, the beginning of a story to be written about a perfect and badly loved protagonist who is like him ("He had thought of everything and everything was in its place, the champagne in the buckets, the guests on the sofas, the cake steeping in its liqueurs, the streamers swaying up to the ceiling, everyone they had known, even those they didn't see any more, he had thought of everything except the fact that she wouldn't come.")

I give him the Château Margaux to open, I turn off the heat under the vegetables and the sauce, I put the filets in the oven to keep them warm, soon there'll be nothing left to worry about, nothing to do but sit down and eat and drink and enjoy the hours ahead until they've melted away.

Lili is humming *Nobody knows you when you're down and out*, though Chet Baker long ago replaced Eric Clapton.

"I suppose you watched the news on television," she says. "That woman, the Place des Arts bag lady."

"I don't know why they leave her there like that," Jean-Eudes says. "It's a shame."

"Terrible," says Thomas.

"What would you like them to do?" Lili asks. "And besides, who are 'they'?"

"She was hiding her face behind her hand to try to get away from the camera," Thomas says. "I would have punched the cameraman in the face."

"I don't understand," Jean-Eudes says, "why they don't force her to stay in a shelter, there's lots of shelters in Montreal, she'd be better off there than in the snow."

"How can you say that?" Lili scolds. "Have you ever set foot in what you call a 'shelter'? Why shouldn't she be able to choose to live all alone, even in the snow, seeing as that's what we have the most of here, snow—and accountants? And furthermore, why should people have to live out their disasters with others, in a filthy shelter, in the midst of losers even more lost than themselves?"

I say I agree with Lili, no one has the right to decide what's good for others, every adult is the master of his own fate, of his scrawny little fate. Lili rolls a joint. Thomas opens another bottle of wine.

"That means," says Jean-Eudes, "that you let suicidal people kill themselves, let junkies do drugs until they're dead, that means you never intervene in people's lives even if you see they're trapped, it means you don't help anybody any more, what fine principles those are."

"You're spitting in my glass, sweetie," Lili says.

"Obviously," says Thomas, "what makes things a bit more complicated here is that we're probably dealing with a former mental patient, or a drug addict."

"So?" Lili says.

"I mean," says Thomas, "that free choice isn't free choice when the person choosing isn't in his right mind, that's what I mean."

"And who's going to decide whether we're in our right minds?" says Lili. "Thomas, do you think you're in your right mind?"

"No," Thomas says, and bursts out laughing. "Especially not now."

"Lili is passionate about bums," says Jean-Eudes. "She is putting together a big piece on bums."

"No," Lili says, giving Jean-Eudes a dark look. "I wanted to, but I gave up on the idea."

"Why?" Thomas asks.

A brief silence, during which she drinks, then sings: *Nobody knows you, nobody...*

"I wanted to become a real bum for a while," Lili says. "I got scared."

"Of course," Jean-Eudes says, stroking her hair. "It's a frightening world."

She shakes her head, gives a throaty little laugh.

"Not that. I was afraid of staying a bum all my life, of never wanting to rejoin the normal world."

She laughs and finishes her glass, and Jean-Eudes laughs too, louder than her. Thomas looks at her intensely, the glass unmoving in his hand. I leap to my feet, called to order by the smell of the grilled marrow.

The bread is cut, the oven turned off, the tournedos covered with sauce, the carrots and zucchini buttered. The biggest helping will be for Lili, as a form of existential consolation.

"How do you do it, Claire?" sighs Lili. "It's so good it makes me sick."

"She doesn't deserve any credit," Thomas says. "She's an alchemist. Everything she touches turns to gold."

"A toast to Claire," says Jean-Eudes.

"To Claire, who is a genius in the kitchen. And with words," Lili says.

"To Claire, who has everything," Thomas says, raising his glass exaggeratedly.

A little longer and the meat would have lost its essential juices, but the cooking was stopped in time, everything melts down and becomes more intense, more itself—the solidity of the foie gras, the smoothness of the marrow, the energy of the red flesh married to the port.

"All the same, it's becoming a problem," says Jean-Eudes.

"The other day a drunk pulled the licence plate off Lili's car."

"It was my fault," Lili says, her mouth full.

"Of course," Jean-Eudes sighs.

"Yes," Lili says. "I was in a hurry, I told him to get lost instead of giving him the quarter he wanted. What would it have cost me to give him a quarter?"

"This fall," Thomas recounts, "I'm sitting in my office, it's five in the afternoon, when a young man knocks at my door and comes in. Seems like a community college student, his face long and sad, very polite. He tells me his mother is dying and he needs twenty-five dollars right away to go to her bedside in Drummondville or Trois-Rivières, I don't remember. He's embarrassed, he has no one to borrow from, his friends have left the city, he shows me his identification, he says he'll pay me back the following Monday. His eyes are hazel—very clear, very honest. I dig through my pockets, I only have two bills, a two and a fifty. I give him the two, I tell him it's all I have, and at the same time I feel totally stingy, like a real asshole."

"Rightly so," Lili says.

"The following Monday," Thomas says, "I found out he had done the same thing to all the teachers in the department."

"Let's be precise," Jean-Eudes says. "He wasn't a bum, he was a thief."

"He was a bum," Thomas said, "a young bum. They use more sophisticated methods to get their money, that's all. More and more of the homeless are young, we have to realize that."

"There's a woman, she's very cunning," says Jean-Eudes, "every year during the holiday season she moves right into the bank. She begs at the exit from the machines, when people are still holding their wallets stuffed with money."

"I can't resist a woman beggar," Lili says, "even if she's a wino, a druggie, and I know she's screwing me around."

I say that, really, a few dollars is a low price to pay to relieve ourselves of some of our guilt feelings.

"What guilt feelings?" Thomas asks. "Do you feel guilty, Claire?"

He opens the bottle of Madrona, Lili lights her second joint.

"Claire thinks everyone is entirely responsible for his fate," Thomas says smiling at me. "She thinks we become what we've really chosen to be. Drunks choose to be drunks, teachers to teach skinheads who tell them to relax their shaft, journalists to write articles on rotten subjects like Rhapsode and Céline Dion. Isn't that right, sweetie, isn't that what you think?"

While taking away the empty plates cluttering the table, I protest that it's not that simple, I've never claimed good or bad luck wasn't a factor in our fate, but there is an autonomous element that people are reluctant to exercise and to...

"She's right," Lili interrupts. "We definitely choose to be the miserable people we are, it's a lot easier to give up than to do anything. For the most part human beings prefer to give up, be accountants, city bureaucrats."

"Thanks," says Jean-Eudes. "Instead of insulting me, love, pass me that joint."

"Dope doesn't agree with you," Lili says, "and you know it. But here, since you want to get sick and pass out, you're the one making the choice, as Claire says."

They're upsetting me. I tell them, laughing, that they're upsetting me, and Lili gets up to kiss me.

"We're teasing you," she says. "We're teasing you because you're right, because you're always right, the beef alone was a terribly delicious proof of your rightness and your mastery of the formless universe. I want to raise my glass again to Claire, Claire who is gifted at everything, and who has everything because she has consciously chosen to have everything."

"To Claire who has everything," Thomas says, "except a suitable boyfriend."

He laughs and moves to clink his glass against the glass of Jean-Eudes, who sways from the contact and lets a few ruby drops fall onto the tablecloth.

"Suitable," Lili says. "There's a word I haven't heard since I was a little child. Suitable, that isn't suitable, these people aren't suitable, who's afraid of Virginia Suitable Woolf?"

"You're loosening up, love," says Jean-Eudes. He struggles to his feet. "What would you say if I sat for a moment in that armchair? It seems to me that the armchair is beckoning me."

"Michael," says Lili. "You all know Michael, don't you?"

"No," Thomas says.

"Yes you do," Lili says. "Michael the hobo, the one who walks the neighbourhood with his black dog and his broken tricycle loaded with old things, sometimes there's even a cat in his trailer..."

"Yes," I say. A little man with thick glasses who keeps his patient black dog on a leash and walks in the middle of the street calling out, *"fucking bourgeois,"* at invisible enemies.

"I haven't seen him," Thomas says.

"There are those who see him," Lili says, "and those who don't. Tourists see him. The other evening, on Laurier, an excited American kept taking his picture. *"Look at the guy, look at the guy, isn't he wonderful?"*

"Ah yes," Thomas says, "I know who you're talking about."

"He's Austrian," says Lili. "He paints, or at least he says he paints. His dog is called Cougar. In the winter he shares a room with someone in the little public housing building across from our place, but in the summer he prefers to sleep in the open air with his stuff, his dog and his tricycle, and to use the Van Houtte toilets for keeping clean."

"Yes." Jean-Eudes's furry voice emerges from his distant armchair. "The old drunk."

"He doesn't drink," Lili says.

"Come on," says Jean-Eudes. "It's obvious that he's always drunk."

"He isn't drunk at all," Lili says, irritated. "Besides, he never smells of alcohol."

"Never?" Thomas says, sardonic.

"I know," Lili says, "I kissed him."

Jean-Eudes straightens up in his armchair. Thomas can't stop laughing.

"Don't look at me like that," Lili says. "Haven't you people ever kissed strangers?"

"Yes," says Thomas, "but not on tricycles."

He starts laughing again, he's doubled over, unable to catch his breath. Lili gives him an indulgent smile.

"It wasn't bad," she says. "And it made him so happy."

"Why did you kiss him?" Jean-Eudes says.

"I was walking along the sidewalk, avenue du Parc. I could hear him behind me, his wheels rattling, him muttering insults."

"*Fucking bourgeois,*" I say.

"Then at the red light we were standing side by side, separated by the space of two bodies. He wasn't looking at me, he never looks at anyone. That's when I said to myself, this guy's a human being, and that's when I spoke to him."

Thomas isn't laughing any more. We are all quietly listening to Lili, Lili who is so beautiful and is speaking with her head tilted back, her eyes elsewhere.

"I talked to him about his dog, I asked him why his dog wasn't with him, if he'd had to get rid of it, and he said, '*Oh no! He's my friend, my old companion!'* His dog was inside, nice and warm, and our conversation was off to a good start, easy, frank, he replied very directly to my questions and had his own to ask in turn, my name, what I did, where I lived, if I was able to keep warm at least, if I was happy, yes, he asked me if I was happy, and we walked like that all along avenue du Parc, then we came to Laurier, and the most striking thing was his dignity, he talked about his 'lifestyle,' he was like an old-fashioned European, civilized, polite, his clothes are clean and well tailored, just a bit out of date, and I was saying to myself, it's incredible, the contrast between the image we have of him, a man in rags, and then suddenly he is so convincing, imperial. Decadent old artist or hobo? In the end it's a thin line between them."

"But in fact," says Jean-Eudes, "this man is totally out of it, he never even stops talking to himself…"

"When we got to the drugstore," Lili says, without paying attention to the interruption, "we separated, because I had some errands to do and in the end we were going to have to go our separate ways, and that's when I kissed him. He was amazed, I can still see his face, his eyes lighting up, and that's when I felt his unhappiness, such a hunger for love came into his eyes, such a lack, suddenly what I had in front of me was a man who for such a long time hadn't felt like a man in front of a woman, he touched my face with his fingers and he moaned, I can still hear his deep sad voice, *"Oh Lili, Lili."*

She relights the joint, which has gone out, and looks towards Jean-Eudes.

"His tongue was very sweet," she says.

She passes the joint to Thomas, then to me. She smiles at me.

"Of course, because he's a man, he's been wanting it ever since, he wants more, he waits for me outside my house almost every day and I have to hide when I see him coming down the street."

"Lili," Jean-Eudes sighs in a low voice.

("He waits all night in front of her place. He doesn't understand. Yesterday she loved him. He remembers very clearly what women in love are like and that's the way she was, yesterday she loved him and today she won't look at him. *Fucking bourgeois*, he says to his dog.")

My hands go out of control on the bowl of cream, the clementine cream I cooked yesterday and which takes so long to beat and to set, and the bowl falls to the floor. It doesn't matter, I'm alone in the kitchen to rinse off the plates, to fill the empty peels one by one with cream, to put them back in the freezer. In an hour they'll be ready to eat with the chocolate truffles, but what will we be up to in an hour? Jean-Eudes has already fallen asleep in the armchair, Lili and Thomas are side by side, drinking port. They don't even look at the cheese I set down in front of them, a Pont-l'Évêque and some creamy Marcelline.

"The question is as follows," Lili says. "What is the exact moment when it happens? When do we slide completely into the blackness, when does the last spark of pride suddenly go out, leaving us ready for anything, for walking filthy and drunk in the street, talking to ourselves and swearing at passers-by? When? Do you know?"

"When," Thomas says, "there is no when, it's an accumulation, day after day, a sequence of defeats, small losses of dignity..."

"But it must have started somewhere," Lili says.

"Yes," says Thomas. "It started one day."

They drink. They don't want watercress salad with mango

and basil vinaigrette. That's good because I've only half pre-pared it.

"I know the answer," Lili says. "It starts when we see we're surrounded by people better than ourselves. That's when it begins."

"I don't know," Thomas says, "maybe."

The truffles, at least. Even if the truffles don't find a taker, they will be there on the table like a happy ending, a reminder that life can also be good and sweet. I suddenly realize that I forgot the truffles in the trunk of the car, the incredibly expensive truffles that have been on their way to freezing for hours. I get up quickly. I tell them I'm going out. I go out.

Outside it is winter. This whole time, without our know-ing it, winter has continued to exist, with its mortal whiteness. The air is pure, as it must have been before life began. At this moment there may be men outside, wrapped in layers of newspapers and clothing, peering into house windows, into the artificial tropics. Truffles in hand, I don't go towards the door, I walk in the snow to feel the cold attacking my feet. At this moment there must be men coming up to windows this way, close enough to see what it is they've been excluded from. Oh I wish all the men could be inside somewhere warm, at this moment I wish it so intensely.

I come up to the window. On the other side are Thomas and Lili. On the other side Thomas and Lili are kissing. They are holding each other very close and they keep on kissing. The scene is amazing, the dramatic situation fabulous, words spring up in me to create a story that is realer than real, but almost immediately the pain comes and strikes the words down, the words go away, I don't have any more words, I don't have anything any more.

HOMELESS

I DON'T yet know that this evening I'll be sitting on a bench in the carré Saint-Louis, beside a wino who stinks without my caring. Normally, winos and I maintain a strategic distance. We know by heart the parts that have been scripted for us: they beg, I give them money. That's where our scene ends. Casting has never entrusted other roles to us. We play the ones we have very well.

I don't know that, this evening, I will give a wino the part of my existence least convertible into money.

For the moment I'm sitting on a cushioned chair and the daylight is filtering into this office which is mine, temporarily. Of course objects are temporary, as are beings. A depressing thought that ruins the taste of wine and other good things. Better to believe that this office lent by the university is definitively mine, just as this section of Saint-Denis that my eyes are catching through the window is mine, and these people, always the same, packed into the glass-fronted cubes of the building across from me.

My office walls are almost bare. But on one of them hangs a picture of a Tuscan window, the shutters half open. I know the window is Tuscan because I am the one who photographed it, in Florence, in a sunlit street where I just happened to be, back when I was another man, burning and unburdened. Seen from below, the wood of the shutters is shot through with translucent pink currents, as if the light had just brought this window into the world, just revealed its raw and beating soul. A silhouette can be seen behind the shutters, immobile at the edge of the light, no doubt disturbed by the intrusion of my looking in, waiting until I leave to begin living again, to lean towards the street's bursting brilliance. Perhaps it's a man, perhaps a woman. Perhaps neither. If you're not careful you can get lost in this picture. On days of great fatigue or powerful hope, the silhouette is a woman smiling at me, full of life, and I can feel the burning of the sun.

I always leave my office door ajar, more out of claustrophobia than out of availability. Students used to flood through it, swamping me with their questions without answers. Now the mistrust is generalized. The students still come but they no longer make waves to get to the source of things. It's not necessarily their fault, or mine.

Someone is knocking. I recognize the soft tapping and the voice coughing from an excess of discretion. He comes in. It's not a student from my class. This one is my son. It can be said of him, honestly and objectively, that he is a good son. Even worse, he is like me.

Every week, after his economics course, he comes to sit in my office for a few minutes. He has a sense of ritual, he always has had, he takes care to conserve the rituals without worrying about the emptiness that accumulates beneath. We have a tired discussion about news items that have grown stale over the past three days. We smoke a few of my cigarettes. He says serious, rational things that are in line with his vision of the world, of the future. One day the Weak will be decimated and the Brilliant will be seated on Power's right. While he speaks, his eyes sadly inspect an unfortunate stain, an unseemly twist in the telephone cord, a pointless doodle on official papers.

My son is a very clean young man. When he goes, an hour later, I'm worn out by his cleanliness and his oldness.

Today he lingers as though searching for an appropriate formula. He ends up admitting to me that he will come to the house tonight for "the occasion." He reddens. He doesn't like birthdays, especially of people close to him. He fears the excesses that force him into others' soft hearts. He only feels good on the outside, where there are no emotions.

My son was a wild little boy. It wasn't I who tamed him.

For a long time I've been searching for the guilty ones. I track the photographs from before, when he was three, eight, fifteen years old. He is between his mother and me, exultant in a filthy pair of overalls. He races his bicycle. He swims. He eats peanuts. He strokes a kitten. And as his childhood passes by on wrinkled photographs, something in his face disintegrates, a light goes out, suddenly he never smiles any more, he looks prematurely broken while we're still laughing, his mother and I, as though we were unconscious. Nothing is more painful for me than looking at these pictures. But they have to be put side by side to establish their relationship and the causes, to examine what happened in the blank spaces. That's where the aggressor is hidden, in the spaces between the photographs.

My son has his own special way of not inquiring about me. He pretends to ask me questions but includes the answers, all of them prepared and tenable: "It's true you don't have too much work right now," "I see you bought yourself a jacket." It would be upsetting to contradict him.

Maybe it hurts him not to love me as much as he would like. Maybe he forces himself to come and sit here every week as a form of expiation.

Now he gets up, holding his hand out as to an official. In

a few years he will use this same ceremonial gesture to take leave of his bosses or subordinates. For a moment I keep his hand in mine, to feel something, to prolong things. His hand is cold and a bit damp.

I could work now. The university pays me to search inside myself and draw out nourishment, new or recycled, for the students to peck at. It's a task of nurturing that grows increasingly hazardous: the food supplies run low and go bad, the cook's hand grows weary of mixing the ingredients.

A colleague's voice reaches me from the adjoining office. I like to hear that voice, unmoving as an object, I like that voice invading me daily to remind me of the world's stability. My colleague and I are within weeks of the same age. For almost twenty years both of us have been trying to teach literature. Literature struggles and continues to live between our stagnant theories, we haven't yet found the way to nail it into place. Even those who've died never finish crying out from their books, and with the passage of time their cries become deafening. Émile Nelligan, Malcolm Lowry, Italo Calvino.

I have had a great love for literature.

Now my colleague waxes indignant over the telephone; then he laughs, he laughs very loudly, entirely taken by the charm of the dialectic. The two of us often play at growing indignant over causes that are worth the bother—Quebec, language, the threat of multiculturalism—and it brings a sort of happy respite, a whiff of extreme youth. Most of the time our indignation is artificial and tired.

When my colleague came into my office last week, for one of our ritual discussions, I suddenly saw his face as a crazy mask, and fixed on a detail so outrageous it made me laugh. The face of my colleague has been invaded by a disturbing hairiness. Gradually his hairs are deserting his skull, but multiplying in his eyebrows and emerging in bushes from his nostrils and his ears. The same ridiculous thing is happening to me. Age is displacing both values and hair. Ridicule won't kill us, my colleague and me; we will be two old men with furrowed cheeks and brows, sagging under triumphant vegetation.

The door is still partly open. A female hand slides in, without knocking. I can do nothing but watch the hand's owner float victoriously to my desk. She sits down. The room fills with the showy warmth of her twenty-two years. We know each other. She has already been in one of my courses, as well as in a terribly obscure zone of my thoughts. This girl is more voracious than beautiful, but the result is the same. Nothing has happened between us, nothing.

I have torn off her clothes while she looked at me with a consenting stare, I have stared at her while she was tearing off her own clothes, she has wrapped herself around me like a fire that both consumes and destroys, I have touched the holy places of her body and songs have welled forth from all her lips, our desire has been a life-giving sword, we have penetrated each other and opened everything up to that ultimate gap through which the soul escapes, never before have I known such unconstrained pleasure.

So many times.

In my thoughts.

She curls into the chair, acts as though she's perfectly at ease. She tells me that she knows today is my birthday, she tells me not to ask her how she knows. From her bag she brings out an object wrapped in tissue paper, and hands it to me. Her eyes say unbearably daring things. I try to avoid her eyes. The object is a book, an illustrated edition of Nelligan's poems. I don't read what she has written on the title page, not right away.

The roundness of beginnings is still in her cheeks, her

hands, which never stop moving, the corners of her lips, still untouched by bitterness. She has barely emerged from childhood yet her powers of seduction are ageless, her way of looking at men as though they were available commodities. These days young women are fearsome warriors.

In all these times that her look has signalled me that we are alone, nothing has happened. Once, in my office, our hands touched and I blushed as though she were naked, and she looked at me as though she wished it too. The next step happened only in my head, the place where we manufacture images to avoid living them.

On the title page she has written, "I invite you to my place between five and seven, or later, or tonight, or whenever you prefer. Happy Birthday."

I've never slept with my students. I would like to have abstained all this time through the largeness of my soul, my visceral faithfulness, sublimation. I wish I could be like the man they see in me, these young woman who offer and demand, I wish the solidity they find so stirring were more than a mirage.

I tell her I won't go. Not this evening, not later. Before leaving she gives me a last chance, the hand she leaves, disillusioned, on my desk, it would suffice to touch it to conjure up the regrets to come. Of course, I don't touch it.

Now that she has left, I see that the day is slowing down, the air is breathable again. I'll have to file this book deep in the library, with those I've already read, perhaps with the title page torn out. Many other lives have passed this way, between my comings and goings. Out of fear, I've always acted as though I didn't see them. One day there will be nothing left to fear, no more alternatives, one day I will see that my life is the only possibility I have.

In a moment the telephone will ring. It's reassuring to know certain things in advance, to keep one's suspicion of immediate reality to a minimum. This evening the sun will set at five forty-five. In a moment my wife will phone me. The Tuscan window, above the telephone, was photographed one day in May, in a state of inconceivable availability, while I—young, stupid and entirely without a protective mask—was exploring the unknown. I wouldn't be able to take that picture now.

The telephone rings. My wife's voice over the telephone sounds incredibly fresh, like a perpetual lie. My wife and I avoided getting married in order to escape being stuck together institutionally. We haven't been married now for twenty-three years. I always say "my wife" because even in French there aren't many words to describe the relations between a greying couple.

As for my wife, I have nothing to complain about. My wife is part of a world that I danced to a few years ago. Agitation, desire and rage, tears of passion, the call to arms against everything mixed together, Quebec and Salvador, the condition of the poor and the welfare of my beloved. The dance of youth.

My wife's voice is as full of life as it used to be when we were burning and in love and driven by a thirst that demanded satisfaction. It is always amazing to hear that same voice commenting on the rise of interest rates.

She talks about my birthday as though it's an annoying disturbance in her otherwise smooth day. Would you prefer to eat at home or at a restaurant? Alone with our son or with a group? Would a new coat be an appropriate present? What time are you thinking of coming home?

Both of us could have started over with someone new—people around us are always starting over in love. So much energy to grasp each other and then let go, to tame each other and then grow tired of knowing each other. Another woman would have had a different way of doing her hair, sharper inflections in her laugh, hands with a softer or rougher touch, unknown or unreasonable ambitions, hair red black blonde frizzed... After a while another woman would no longer be new.

My wife says the prime minister is leading us straight into economic disaster. My wife says it snowed in San Diego. Those are the things peace is made of, that sequence of small certainties that paves the road before us: otherwise, how can we go forward without stumbling, how can we not be swallowed up by the horizon? My wife and I keep each other from falling into the unknown.

Now I'm outside. Here things are more uncertain. It's the fault of this anarchic crowd, a scattering of contradictory identities moving about inharmoniously, with no common goal. Students greet me. But a few steps farther and I almost cease to exist, the street swallows the students and mixes them up with everyone else, illiterates and vagrants.

I go up Saint-Denis as slowly as a heart patient or a drunk. Saint-Denis has a lot of drunks. Winos. Vagrants. Homeless. The words to name them are starting to proliferate as their invasion becomes more conspicuous, a new visible minority, urban gangrene. The winos are ugly. They stink. They look us in the eyes as though we were responsible for what's happening to them.

One of them is shuffling about near a parking meter, looking for fallen change. He goes like that from one meter to the next, unhurried, like a Sunday stroller, like an unbeliever sluggishly following the stations of the cross. The looks of the passers-by rise curiously towards him, but nothing seems to bother him, he is beyond all that, curiosity and indifference.

Passing near him, I drop a quarter, as though by accident.

Immediately he puts his foot on it. Farther along I stop, near another meter, to observe him. The quarter has disappeared into his pocket. He glances in my direction, letting out subterranean mumblings. When his eyes are on me I drop another coin, underlining my gesture. He sees it. He looks at me. His eyes are of no particular colour, except where the blood has pooled. I move to the next meter. There's no name for this game I have just invented, no name that can be admitted.

Now we are both motionless in front of our meters, on the lookout while the moving horde curves angrily around us. Stationary beings are suspect. Looking him in the eyes, I throw down a loonie. He doesn't understand. He accepts not understanding. He picks up the coin while staring at me as though hypnotized. Then he follows me from meter to meter, old Tom Thumb tottering with stupefaction. Slowly we make our way up Saint-Denis. Now I'm dropping two-dollar and five-dollar bills. Every time I look around, he's staying at a respectful distance. He looks at me. No one has ever looked at me this way, with so much hope.

Now we are near the carré Saint-Louis. I cut towards the park, plunge far beyond the pavilions, into the amber evening light. I am looking for a bench that might be waiting for me in the darkness, but there is no darkness anywhere.

I sit down. He stands a bit back, swaying from leg to leg so the fatigue is equally shared. Patient and mystified, he's waiting to see what happens next. He would like something to happen next. His face is turned to me, alive with wanting. At this moment I would give anything for something or someone to possess some of this power over me, the power to rekindle the old wild desires sealed beneath the plaster. At this moment my wife and my son are uncorking a bottle of Bruno Paillard, they aren't yet worried.

He sits down at the end of the bench. He's an ordinary

drunk, ruined by alcohol. Age indeterminate, but near the end. I give him what little remains inside my wallet. Then I give him the wallet itself, the keys to my car, my watch, my briefcase, my leather tie, my sheepskin gloves, my ring. He snatches each object as it's offered, with silent desperation, panicky at the idea that my madness may suddenly stop before he's gotten as much as possible out of it.

I would give him more, I would give him everything I am and everything that weighs on me, if these things could be transferred. At this moment my wife and my son are sipping the Bruno Paillard and consulting their watches.

I ask him for a drink. He offers me a mickey of gin, he calls me his brother. We toast. For a long time we remain side by side, tamed, comparing wounds. He laughs, I laugh with him, then I cry, he cries with me. Brother.

When I look up I see the window. It's a wood-framed window in the Tuscan style, its shutters are half open and the memory is so powerful that it is staring me right in the face. The light from rue Laval brushes the shutters and sends translucent pink currents of light shooting across them. And exactly as in my Florentine photograph, a silhouette appears behind the shutters, motionless at the edge of the light. The silhouette comes to life, leans out the window, towards the street. I stand up, I recognize Émile Nelligan in his shirt with its old-fashioned collar. He looks at me compassionately and seems to call something out to me, but what?… What?…

WHITE

SINCE WE first met, Mr. Murphy, I have hardly slept. As soon as I leave your room, I go into a state of overexcitement very far from the contemplative mood you should inspire in me. When I manage to calm down, I dream that men I don't know are puncturing me with their tireless phalluses without satisfying me in any way, leaving me bubbling like a suppressed volcano unable to expel its lava. I am not good, Mr. Murphy. I want to live like an animal even if I am watching you die.

I'm sorry that's all I have to offer you, a magma of feverish and tyrannical desires, I'm sorry to be the woman you depend on in your final moments. I haven't always been this way, you should have met me before, years before I left and then returned to Montreal, my suitcases stuffed with frenzy and panic.

Montreal has changed, it's Montreal's fault. Just two years away and now I've lost my landmarks, now I run around nose to the ground, senses on the alert, a disoriented dog searching for familiar smells. Just two years and now when I look in the mirror I can no longer find my youth. Montreal was family, Montreal was a nice reassuring dump where there was nothing to fear except English assimilation, Montreal just had some old quarrels about fences to keep harping on and I detested that, Mr. Murphy, I liked to detest that and I longed for other cities with more interesting wars. Maybe since the referendum, when you yourself, on your feet then and glowing with health, in all likelihood voted against the accession of the

French fact in America, maybe since the outcome of the referendum, Montreal has subtly lost its defensive provincialism, along with its cause, and gradually, without my noticing, clothed itself in the hard shell that true cities wear, the cities where you have to learn to become someone all alone, with no patriotic support.

The old Montreal kept me a child; since my return I run around and sleep around and drink too much, looking for the old Montreal whose comfortable narrowness I used to find so depressing.

I don't recognize my friends now. Several have become Buddhists. It's because of them that I spend all these hours sitting beside you, awkwardly absorbing your shivers of pain, it's because of the books they carelessly dropped in my path, knowing I've always been vulnerable to words that make the silence speak.

We won't last, Mr. Murphy.

That's what the silence says, whenever there's a gap in the racket and roar.

We won't last, ourselves, our so blond so brown so likeable so combative selves who make love and Beef Wellington with the same intensity, who go to sleep every night miraculously convinced we will wake up, our cherished selves, our sheltered treasure in its quivering intimacy and its emotions that are so alive.

What a nasty surprise, Mr. Murphy.

We should have listened to the silence more often.

Even here, even penetrated by this implacable truth, even near you, like being at a dress rehearsal, in the clouds of terror that you exhale and I feel in my gut, a part of me wants to remain deaf and ignorant, a huge part of me rebels and says, not me, you and the others maybe, but not me.

I like honesty, Mr. Murphy; I write books, and books that

lie aren't worth the paper they're printed on, I am with you to destroy that stubborn part of myself that panics in the face of honesty and denies the naked truth.

You have no idea of the maze I plunged into in order to reach you. I had to agree to open, one by one, the doors of this *Tibetan Book of the Dead*, the very reading of it leaves one disturbed for ever after, and behind each one of those doors you were waiting for me without knowing it. In this terrifying book it is said that there is no generosity greater than accompanying a human being into his death, at the precise moment when the living no longer consider him one of their own, and abandon him to his personal hell. But I am not a generous woman. If I'm here it's because I need you even more than you need me.

I put myself onto the lists of volunteers, in these places specializing in palliative care, care that doesn't restore health because there's no more health to be restored. I made sure not to seem too eager, because eagerness is much more frightening than indifference, I didn't play at being a mystic because I was afraid of not knowing the right lines, but I demonstrated such calm insistence that they registered me in a course, along with twenty-five equally suspect aspirants to goodness, and for an intolerable number of hours we had to listen to geriatric specialists, psychiatrists and spiritual guides advising us on how best not to harm you.

I am ashamed, Mr. Murphy, I am ashamed of thinking I could attend your death as easily as an educational show, I am ashamed of having believed you would remain anonymous until the end.

I had prepared myself for the most terrible sights but when I went into your room for the first time I was shocked. You were stretched out on your bed, of course, your skin so pale it was almost transparent, and when I introduced myself you turned your very blue eyes towards me: "*Oh, a French chick,*" you murmured in your sardonic voice, and I saw you weren't even old, not old and not in agony, hardly more dying than me when I'm recovering from the flu or drinking too much, and I suddenly understood that I would have to accompany a living man on this terrifying journey, not a dried-up inanimate carcass, not a hypothetically human otherworldly mask, but a person as alive as myself.

We quickly touched hands, and you saw the disturbance in my eyes at the same time as I saw something disconcerting and joyous light up in yours. You found me unexpected too, Mr. Murphy. The nurses had told me about your belligerent misanthropy, your anger when people tried to comfort you or make contact. I wasn't what your irritated self dreaded and hoped for, I should have been more like the sober image we have of charity, in dull clothes and filled with pieties. But that evening I was the way I've been for months, tortured by the desire to explode, and I never wear dull clothes, which eclipse the body instead of allowing it to shine.

We have each been as disarmed as the other, Mr. Murphy, because instead of courageously peering into the sacred country of death, we've both been resolutely clinging to the side of life—a very mediocre team, you have to admit, for confronting what is coming.

That night, while you were trying to sleep but only dozing fitfully, I was aflame. I criss-crossed Montreal, searching for someone to burn with me, but it was a boring and deserted Monday, and I ended up telephoning a man I was once in love with, a long time ago, and he miraculously turned out to be free, or a quick enough liar to invent an excuse to float from his marriage bed to mine.

When the night was over he left as early as possible. Unlike my old friends, this man had changed very little, his body and his feverish way of expressing sexual passion were sufficiently the same to send me back thousands of days into the past, but I didn't find that comforting. Neither the stagnation of the motionless nor the advance of those who change can reassure me, there is no security anywhere, anywhere.

The next day, Mr. Murphy, we talked about love. You had traded in your hospital gown for a set of purple silk pyjamas—in my honour, no doubt. You tried out a few words of French, that losers' dialect you never wanted to master even living in Montreal, but that wore you out quickly. And soon words of any language seemed insufficient to you, and you showed me some pictures.

It's one of the only things you kept from your life, a hundred or so methodically ordered pictures in an envelope, and while I went through them you watched my reactions with that defiant edge your grin always had back then, but I let nothing slip, I leafed through those hundred snapshots of women with their sparkling beautiful faces as though they were a column of articles for sale or rent among which I might find a windfall. In those pictures of women, each alone, each different from the others, I was searching for you. They were dressed modestly but unclothed where it counts, naked in their expressions of pure supplication, their expressions of unloved lovers. And then finally I found you, barely younger than you are now, smiling, handsome and robust, accompanied not by a woman but by a horse you were holding by the bridle.

I knew you were a collector, Mr. Murphy, I knew it as soon as I came into your room, and maybe even before, in that unconscious pool from which all our deeds arise I have always been attracted by collectors of women, as by an obliterating black hole, and I always expect those men to stop doing, for my sake, what attracted me to them. We are two starving creatures of irreconcilable species, and the starving are indeed condemned to gallop in parallel lines, to use a horsey metaphor that becomes you, Mr. Murphy, condemned in their demented search to lose everyone along the way and end up alone at the place where they were so sure they would be accompanied.

That's what we talked about.

You gave me the pictures, asking me to destroy them, and this gesture of confidence taught me that you had, alas, ceased to be a stranger, and I asked if I could keep the one of you with the horse, the one that shows your real sexual preferences. You laughed, and that's the only time I've heard you laugh.

For a few days I went into your room the way we go into a café, spurred on by the certainty of finding the density of life and the nicotine of conversation, but our conversations were like a priceless liqueur, viscous, unfiltered, without preliminary, and they dropped into my mind like volcanic rocks that have burned off their useless slag, and remained there going round and round interminably. I confided to you that I'd fled my mother's death, then my father's, fled like a coward both times, rejecting their desperate eyes and stinking agony, and you told me the cowardly things you had done, which were no less than mine and all had to do with women. What bizarre meetings, Mr. Murphy, "What a strange blind date," you would sigh, wrapping me in the blueness of your eyes, because we didn't always talk, often we held hands with a warmth so sensual that afterwards you would be in my dreams, yes, you were among those dream lovers agitating my nights without succeeding in satisfying me.

Absurdly, I got to the point where I forgot why I was with you; and you, at my touch, shone with the misleading brilliance that supernovas have before they explode. But the seventh day, when I came into your room, I couldn't find you, you had suddenly fallen into a semicoma and started to leave your body.

I resented that as a profound betrayal, I was so angry at you for leaving me stranded after tricking me with your illusions, that I swore at you, you fucking Anglo egomaniac, then, my heart cold with anger, I went to the elevator, where without warning the white faces of my father and mother were waiting for me, their ghost faces returned from non-existence to put a stop to my irreparable desertions.

I went back to your room, Mr. Murphy, and sat down while you slowly disintegrated.

So it's all held in place by a thread—beauty, the harmonious organization of our faces and our bodies that we offer to others like bouquets of eternity—so much care and make-up for such a precarious mask. I look at you, but then sometimes I can't look, and I leave you again, for shorter and shorter times, to relieve my attacks of fever in quick walks along Saint-Denis or Sainte-Catherine, to drink and lose myself for a moment in a quick union with a warm and living body. My desires are the kind that must consume themselves to disappear, and I consume them one by one, and I come back to you more detached each time, I promise you, a little stronger each time to bear your own detachment.

Yesterday you woke up suddenly and asked me, with such terror that my heart stopped beating, *"Where am I going?"*

There is no god in your personal mythology, no paradise waiting at the end of your days, but something in you longs to go on, and no doubt something of us will go on, Mr. Murphy; but until we're dead we can't know the exact details. Whatever goes on, let's let it go on, and let's let the rest sleep—that's what I told you, with a lightness that's not like me, it arrived like an inspiration from your fear, and it was the right thing to say to you, I'm sure, because an ironic flame appeared in the faded blue of your eyes, a flame of your own lightness. Yes, lightness is the way for you to go, the most likely way to go smoothly where you have to go, lightness is what we most lack in this leaden life where all we know is how to pour our anxieties into the miraculous universe, miraculously empty.

Now it's snowing, a snow you can no longer see because you've fallen back into your inexorable dissolution, and I am trembling with cold at your bedside, burdened by sorrow and fear. I'm not crying, because no obstacle should block your passage towards space, but I read you these lines in a low voice as a prayer for you and a lullaby for myself. In a little while, when you have completely escaped the shell that has grown so cumbersome, when you are no longer an Anglophone or a Montrealer or a man but volatile essence set free from the darkness, for a moment I myself will feel like virgin space, John, like you I will be a white page on which nothing has been written.